AFIA IN THE LAND OF WONDERS

AFIA IN THE LAND OF WONDERS

WRITTEN AND ILLUSTRATED BY
MIA ARAUJO

SCHOLASTIC PRESS / NEW YORK

Library of Congress Cataloging-in-Publication Data available

ISBN 978-1-338-85672-9

10 9 8 7 6 5 4 3 2 1 25 26 27 28 29

Printed in China 38
First edition, April 2025

Book design by Omou Barry

For my twin sister, Barbra

1

THE MARKET

Afia raced past the caravan tents, feeling alive. Market day was the only day each month that she and the other citizens of Dafra were allowed a glimpse of the outside world. Around her, vendors wearing bold, colorful patterns bartered with the buyers from Dafra, who dressed in white. The aroma of spices and simmering meat filled the air. There were intricately woven rugs and tapestries for sale, baskets bursting with all kinds of fruits and vegetables, and countless treasures fashioned from iron, silver, and gold. Everywhere Afia looked, she was met with wonders.

"Afia, wait!" Aya called after her. Aya was Afia's twin sister, but because of her confident nature, everyone treated her like she was older. "You won't believe what I just found," she said, showing Afia her prize—small cakes of sweet, fermented rice.

Afia took one and ate it with a laugh. "What would I do without you?"

"He tried to sell me old ones because he thought I wouldn't know any better," Aya told her. "But our ewende is tomorrow. We're practically adults already."

Afia's smile faded. Tomorrow, all the sixteen-year-olds in Dafra would be initiated into adulthood and inherit their family's trade. But Afia was not ready for any of that. She wanted to hold on to this last moment of childhood.

Afia noticed a young boy watching them, looking back and forth at their faces. He ran up and pointed to Aya. "If I pinch you, will she feel it?"

Afia looked away in annoyance. All their lives, she and Aya had endured the same tired questions about whether they had their own secret language or if they could read each other's minds. Aya seemed to enjoy the attention, especially after their mother had explained that some people believed that twins were a sign of good fortune. But this only made Afia feel like even more of an oddity.

Before Afia had a chance to respond, the boy made a lunge for the raffia bag slung over her shoulder.

Aya swatted his hand away. "That's not yours! What would your maame think if she knew what you were up to?"

The startled boy scampered off, disappearing into a group of giggling children.

"You're too trusting, Afia. Remember what our maame always says—you never know who might possess magic. Even a little boy like that." Aya ran a hand over Afia's braids. "Come on. The market will be closing soon. We have a lot left to see!"

Hand in hand, the sisters continued on. They passed weavers, tailors, and metalsmiths, as well as jewelers from all over Djiombé. Some merchants had traveled through the Kuruujiita Desert to the north, some came from the mountainous kingdom of Nyasi, and some had even sailed from across the Sumayan Seas. It made Afia feel proud that Dafra was known in such distant places.

Afia and Aya's parents owned a small crystal mine that had been in the family for generations, and they set up shop alongside the other Dafran vendors. Aya had fought to get their parents to allow them an hour's worth of unsupervised browsing. Their mother had eventually relented, on the condition that they help at the family stall for the rest of the market.

A large man in brilliant blue robes beckoned the sisters toward cages filled with colorful birds. "A parrot for a pair of princesses!" he crowed. "This one is as clever as you are and can even hold a conversation. Go on, tell him your name."

"We have no use for such nonsense," Aya said, dragging her sister away. "How would we even care for such a beast?"

Afia said nothing but gazed back until the magnificent birds disappeared from view. Her disappointment was driven away by a familiar face—an elderly woman tending a cart filled with weathered volumes and scrolls.

"Fatou!" The sisters greeted her.

"Look at you, Aya," said Fatou. "Ever the elegant young lady." She grinned at Afia, offering her a tattered book. "You'll like this one, child. It's Kadiri the Navigator's account of his travels across Djiombé and beyond. Plenty of drawings too!"

Afia opened the book eagerly. A Mbéle man in colorful robes played the kora, surrounded by people sipping mint tea. There were several drawings of birds that Afia had never seen before, from every part of Djiombé, as far as the Uboran coast. And even further into the book, strangely costumed men and women gazed back at Afia from behind their jeweled masks. They moved gracefully through stone palaces and extravagant gardens, seeming to dance as she flipped the pages.

If only my family's trade would let me travel, she thought. But Afia had never revealed this longing to anyone. Her parents and grandmother would laugh at her, and then double her chores. She even kept it secret from Aya. Their sameness defined them; it always had. If she were to tell Aya about everything that she wished she could see and experience beyond Dafra, it would be like speaking their differences into being, and she was afraid of what might happen, of what would change between them.

"For you, little flower, only two gold pieces," said Fatou.

Afia looked at her sister.

"We can't fit any more of your books under my bed," Aya warned. "And you know what Maame will do if she finds them. Besides, I thought we were going to get you something to wear for our ewende." Aya sighed when she saw the look on Afia's face. "Go on, then. You can borrow something of mine."

Afia threw her arms around her sister.

"You two are going to be women soon, is that it?" The old woman smiled as she took Afia's gold.

"That's right," Aya said proudly. "The next time you see us, Fatou, we'll be proper crystal merchants."

Afia opened her book again. She didn't want to think about selling crystals, or dealing with customers, or the many ways that she would undoubtedly disappoint her mother. She let Aya lead her away as she turned the pages. She wondered where such oddly dressed people came from, what they were like, and what kinds of conversations they had. Did they have to do chores and attend ceremonies as well, or did they do whatever they liked? She flipped to a scene where they were playing some strange outdoor game, hitting a ball through hoops with a large wooden hammer.

"Aya, look at this—" Afia began, but her sister was not there. Only a moment ago, Aya had been right in front of her. Now Afia was alone in a sea of strangers. The sounds of the market began to close in around her.

Afia called her sister's name. The people closest to her began to stare. A vendor approached, thrusting a string of beaded jewelry in her face. "Amber beads, coral beads, lapis lazuli!" Behind her, the slam of the fishmonger's knife made Afia jump. A pile of fish heads stared at her, their mouths agape.

Afia backed away into a large woman holding several bolts of fabric. "Watch where you're going, girl!" the woman shouted. Afia stammered an apology and fled. The once-wonderful market now teemed with judgmental faces. She was lost without her sister, and she was certain that everyone around her knew it.

Afia escaped the center of the market and found a quieter row of stalls. A gleam of orange light caught her eye. In front of her stood a tent that she had never seen before, hung with desert-worn rugs and fabrics. The soft jingle of lamps swaying on silver chains and the gentle aroma of incense hung in the air. Spread among tea sets and smoking pipes lay dozens of wooden animal carvings—lions, elephants, monkeys, and birds of all kinds.

Overcome by curiosity, Afia paused to admire each one, studying their graceful curves and bold shapes. Then she discovered the source of the strange light—a row of wooden figures, each with a piece of amber set into its carved-out center. The translucent stones caught and refracted light in oranges and golds. She could even see insects trapped in some of them.

As Afia bent in for a closer look, she bumped the edge of the table. A giraffe figure fell and hit the ground with a crack.

A tall, slender young man, perhaps a few years older than herself, was sitting on the other side of the table watching her with his dark eyes. He wore an embroidered tunic, and a large gold earring gleamed in one ear.

Afia's face grew warm. Her sister was not there to save her. "I'm so sorry," she said, reaching into her bag for gold. "Please tell the carver that it was an accident."

The young man rose and walked over to her. "I *am* the carver."

Afia stared at the floor. She wished she were anywhere else, even at one of Master Fọlámí's lectures on ancient scripture.

"Mistakes are not to be feared," the young man said softly. "I have made many myself." He bent to retrieve each piece of the broken giraffe. "Watch this." He took out a small knife and, with only a few strokes, carved a gazelle from the largest of the pieces. "You see? There is no tragedy where there is transformation." The figure seemed to come to life in his hand, prancing and tossing its head.

Afia gasped. "Did it just move?"

The young man smiled. "You tell me."

The gazelle figure stood motionless where he had left it. Surely, she had imagined it. "How did you learn to make all of these?" she asked.

"Years of dedication. Taking ordinary wood and seeing the potential inside, waiting to be revealed—that is the most satisfying part."

Afia marveled at the elegant shapes of his carvings. He seemed too young to be so skilled . . . Granted, he was from a different land. Come to think of it, she could not remember seeing him with the caravan before. Perhaps wherever he came from, artisans began their training as small children. Afia was too shy to ask.

"That hornbill you are looking at," the young man said suddenly. "Is it your favorite?" He continued, not

waiting for her reply, "Are you sure you wouldn't prefer the lion, or perhaps the leopard?" He picked up each one in turn. "Those were the most difficult to make. I carve these from life, you see."

"These are real animals?" Afia asked.

"You've never seen a leopard before?" The young man held the figure close to her face.

"No." Afia drew back. "I've never seen any of these creatures. It is forbidden to leave Dafra."

"Not one? A leopard or lion, I can understand; they are as dangerous as they are beautiful. But a forest elephant? Or a hornbill? My dear girl, you are not living if you have never set your eyes on such creatures."

"Well, I did just see a parrot back there," Afia said quietly. There was a look of pity on the young man's face. She felt embarrassed, both for never having seen any of these animals and for her longing to talk to this stranger, to hear about the things he had seen.

"I've traveled through deserts and deep forests, across the savannah, and beyond," the young man said. "There are creatures out there so rare and wonderful that you would think I invented them. Seeing them through my carvings is one thing, but you must experience their grandeur for yourself . . ." A sudden smile brightened the young man's face as he closed his hands over hers. "Come with me," he said.

Afia stared. "What?"

"I'm serious! I can be your guide." The look of horror on her face must have been comical, because the young man laughed. "Only the curious are truly alive. Trust me. When you've seen the sights I have seen, you'll want to share them with everyone too."

Afia stumbled backward, slipping her hand out of his grasp. She turned and collided with her sister.

"Afia, you can't run off like that!" Aya put an arm around her and glared at the young man. "Who are you?"

"Only a simple carver," the young man said, "happy to share his creations." He regarded them both for a moment. "Sisters, I presume."

"You're an observant one," Aya scoffed.

The young man laughed softly and returned his attention to Afia. He placed the gazelle into her hands. "A gift. But if you decide you'd rather see the real thing, meet me here at midnight." He gave her one last smile and turned away, disappearing beneath the flapping fabric of his tent.

Afia stared after him, not daring to look at Aya. She squeezed the gazelle so tightly that the pulsing in her hands made her feel for a moment that the small figure had a heartbeat of its own, and that with hers, they pulsed as one.

2

THE CRYSTAL STALL

The sisters walked back to their parents' tent, silence hovering between them. Afia slipped the gazelle figurine into her market bag and glanced at her sister. Aya was rarely silent about what she disapproved of, so Afia knew that she must be furious to not say anything at all.

Finally, Aya turned to face her. "Not a word about that to Maame, understand? It never happened."

Afia nodded. If her mother found out that she had even considered the boy's offer, she would have thrown

Afia out of the house immediately. Her mother valued loyalty above all else and would have seen Afia's hesitation as an insult—an attack on her pride as a parent. She owed it to her mother, Afia told herself, to set her dreams aside. After all, every Dafran child knew exactly who they would be when they grew up. Obeneba would become a weaver, their neighbor Ejiro, a metalsmith. Afia and Aya would sell crystals like their mother and Nana Musu before her. Afia had never even thought to ask her mother if she had ever wanted to do something else with her life.

As they reached the family tent, their mother, Thema, looked up. Her beautiful face was framed severely by a white head wrap, two enormous gold earrings, and a heavy silver necklace. "There you are, my dears, what treasures did you find for me? Surely you didn't forget to find a new stool, as I asked you to." Her smile faded as she noticed their empty hands. She turned to her husband. "Ime! Your daughters wasted a full hour! Didn't I tell you?"

Their father, a timorous, prematurely aged man,

was busy with a potential buyer. His beard was mostly gray, and his turban hid the small amount of hair left to him. He smiled nervously at his wife but said nothing. Thema huffed and turned back to her daughters. "Did you two wander about with your eyes closed?"

At this, the buyer glanced up at Afia and Aya, before returning his gaze to the display with a slight shake of his head. Afia longed to disappear.

Aya stepped forward. "I was disappointed by the market this time, Maame. Everything we saw was a mockery of your taste. The vendors must have sold everything good on their last stop."

Thema seemed satisfied by this. "*We* should be the first stop for the caravan, not Mbéle. How many times have I told the elders this? Come on, then, help your poor mother pack up for the evening, hm? You can start with those crystals over there."

As her mother turned her attention toward the buyer, Afia realized that she had been clenching her jaw. She relaxed it slowly.

Thema shooed her husband away, ordering him to go buy fish before the market closed. "And how are you, kind traveler?" she asked the buyer in a silky voice. "You've come to the place that sells the clearest Dafran crystals. You seem like a man of exquisite taste. Perhaps these fine goblets are what you are looking for? Go on, feel the weight of them. This is true quality. Quality that will last generations."

Afia admired her mother's ease with strangers. Thema's dark eyes followed the buyer's every gesture, analyzing his weaknesses. She was a natural—or at least, she had worked very hard to be—and whenever she sent their father away, Afia knew it was because her mother recognized a potential sale. And she had not been wrong this time.

"Afia, darling, wrap these up for this good man, will you?" Thema gestured at the goblets.

As her mother took a bag of gold from the man and made pleasantries, Afia began to wrap his purchase in cloth.

"No, not like that," her mother scolded. "You're going to break it. Carefully. Turn it over. No, the other way. The *other* way. Can't you see which way I'm pointing? Use your head, girl!" She pushed Afia aside and began to wrap the cup, aggressively but deftly.

Afia met the buyer's eyes for a second time and saw pity there, or perhaps disapproval.

"What are you standing there for?" her mother snapped. "Get back to helping your sister." Afia hurried away and heard her mother say to the man, "It's like my own mother always says, if you want something done right, you have to do it yourself."

Aya motioned for Afia to help hoist a large crystal onto the cart. "Don't let her get to you. That's just how she is. But if you stand there gaping like that, people will start to gossip."

The buyer thanked Thema and turned to Afia with a smile. "Here you are, girl." He tossed her a small gold piece. "For your help," he said, before disappearing into the crowd.

Afia beamed as she showed her family the kind man's coin.

"You could've gotten another if you'd wrapped it properly," her mother said.

Afia put the coin into her bag gloomily. So this was the future that her ancestors had decided for her—being berated by her mother until the day she died.

Her thoughts suddenly returned to the young man from the caravan, and to his offer. What wonders had he seen that must be so urgently shared? And what had prompted him to extend such an invitation to her of all people? Aya was usually the one whom people were drawn to, yet even after meeting her sister, the young man had made his offer to her, not to Aya.

Afia's mind flickered through the possible explanations, but none satisfied her. All she knew was that the young man had looked at her in a way that no one in Dafra ever had. It baffled her. But it also excited her.

3

THE SPARK

The Dafrans made their way home on foot along a narrow road, descending from the cliffs into the streets below. Their town had been carved centuries ago into this cliffside valley, so it was said, by a group of wanderers who had traveled westward across Djiombé, through deserts and dense rainforests. Many had been lost along the way, perhaps attacked by wild beasts or tricked away by spirits, no one knew for certain. But after months of journeying, the Dafran people had come upon an empty valley flanked on one side by fertile fields and sparse trees and on the other by an ominous expanse of forest.

That untamed wilderness had unnerved Afia's ancestors, but the thought of building their home far from the envious eyes of the outside world was irresistible. As they had chiseled deeper into the cliffs, they discovered vast veins of crystal and ore. And thus, the basis of their new society was born—they farmed the fertile land above the valley and mined the precious stones below. Careful to protect their way of life, they limited their contact to the few traders and merchants approved by the Dafran elders.

Aya grabbed Afia's hand, breaking her out of her thoughts. "Don't let Maame get to you," she said. "Nobody can do anything right in her eyes."

Afia smiled. Her sister always knew how to calm her. Afia felt lucky that she had been born with her best friend. That she was never truly alone.

Obeneba, the bully, was watching her and Aya. He strode toward them. "What's it like having a mirror with you all day?"

The young people closest to them began to giggle and nod.

Obeneba spoke louder. "Can your parents even tell you apart, or do they just yell out a name and see who answers?"

Everyone laughed. Aya laughed too, but Afia knew that this was her sister's way of distracting others from how uncomfortable she was.

Afia did not join them in laughing. She was tired of hiding how she really felt. She was tired of being reminded that she and Aya were not normal, that most people saw them as the same person, split into two bodies. She wished that they would see her as more than a mere echo of her sister, who excelled over her in every way.

Afia stormed away down the cliffside steps, afraid of what she might say if she stayed.

Aya's playful voice followed her. "Come on, I'll race you!"

Afia laughed as her sister sped past her, and she forgot about Obeneba's words. As she ran, another voice returned to her suddenly, causing her to slow down. *When you've seen the sights I have seen, you'll want to share them with everyone too.* Afia steeled herself against the visions that these words conjured—wondrous trees and plants, fanciful creatures, and people with all sorts of stories and ideas. She had different dreams than Aya—she wanted a life that she could never have in Dafra.

Aya was waiting for her at the bottom of the steps. "You let me win. What's wrong? You're not yourself today." She took Afia's hand between both of hers. "Don't worry about tomorrow. I'll be right there with you."

Afia nodded. She didn't want Aya to know what she had been thinking about. She stared out over the stone streets, the stone houses, and the crystals catching the last light of the day in their many facets. Her eyes came to rest on the small patch of darkening sky, framed on all sides by the soaring cliffs above. It felt like watching a window slowly being shut. One that would never open again.

Later that evening, while fetching bowls for the family dinner, Afia glanced at the calabash that her mother used to store dried fruit. She noticed that the lid was askew and something gleamed from within. Instead of fruit, there lay two crystal combs, waiting for the ceremony tomorrow. Her favorite part of the ewende was when the parents presented their newly initiated child with a gift made from the family trade. Some parents offered tools, weapons, or jewelry. Thema had clearly chosen this gift because she knew how much her daughters loved to braid each other's hair.

Afia quickly put the lid back.

"No peeking," Nana Musu said, lightly whacking Afia with her broom.

Afia laughed nervously. "Peeking at what?"

"That's right," her grandmother tutted. "Now get a move on with those bowls, girl, or we'll have to eat your mother's soup off the table."

Aya, Thema, and Ime entered the room, carrying a

feast between them. There was rice, plantains, and Afia's favorite, a palm nut soup with fish that they only had on market day. Aya knelt at the table and elegantly poured wine for the adults as their mother and grandmother sat on their floor cushions.

"Afia, will you serve the soup, please?" her mother said. Afia had served her family a hundred times before, but tonight her hands trembled, spilling more soup onto the table than into any of the bowls.

Her father took the serving bowl from her hand gently and wordlessly urged her to sit as he cleaned up the spill.

"Ime!" her mother scolded him. "How will she ever learn if you do everything for her?"

Smiling merrily, Ime set a steaming bowl of soup in front of his wife. "Let her be a child for one more night, eh?"

Afia managed a smile. She admired her father's fortitude in the face of judgment. When her bowl arrived, the aroma of pepper and spices drowned out everything else.

"Straight to bed after this, hm?" Thema said, eyeing her daughters. "I need you to be fresh so you remember every step."

The sisters murmured their agreement. Afia watched as her mother tore the fufu on her plate into smaller and smaller pieces.

"Remember," Thema went on, as though they hadn't heard it a dozen times already from Master Fọlámí, "you are not to greet the masked dancer until *after* you have received the elders' blessing."

Nana Musu cleared her throat, and everyone leaned in to listen. "Take care not to embarrass your mother tomorrow. You must make her proud."

To Afia's surprise, her mother's face brimmed with emotion. "I am already proud," Thema said. "Of both of my daughters."

Afia couldn't remember ever being the object of her mother's pride. She set her spoon down, feeling sick. All her life, she had gone along with her mother's wishes, because that was what Dafran children did. As far as her mother knew, selling crystals was exactly what Afia wanted because it was what Aya wanted. Afia had hidden her dreams so well that she had managed to earn her mother's admiration. But she had earned it for the wrong reason.

"The ewende," Afia began. "I don't want to—"

Her mother did not look up as she carefully spooned more plantains onto her plate. "What don't you want?"

Afia opened her mouth and closed it again.

"Speak up," her mother said tersely. "Is there something you want to say? Out with it. Did I raise a coward or a woman?"

Afia considered herself more of a coward out of the two options, and this realization angered her. "I don't want to be initiated tomorrow," she said. "I don't want to work with crystals. And I don't want to stay in Dafra for the rest of my life." She looked down, ashamed. When she looked up, she saw a wounded expression on her mother's face.

"What *do* you want?" asked Thema.

When she did not answer, her mother raised her voice. "You started this conversation, Afia. I'm giving you the chance to speak for yourself. What could you possibly want that's more important than our family?"

Afia stared into her soup. She knew that no words could answer such an accusation.

"All *I* want for you and your sister is a future," her mother said loudly. "All of us have worked hard to make sure the two of you grew up in comfort. If I had known that you wanted something *else*, then I wouldn't have bothered working for the past sixteen years to transform that miserable crystal mine into one of the most profitable trades in all of Dafra. All you have to do tomorrow is inherit it and avoid running it into the ground. *You* can do that, can't you?" Thema looked sharply at Aya, who nodded vigorously.

"You see?" her mother continued. "Your sister understands what it means to be obedient and grateful. I think those are admirable traits, but who knows? Maybe I'm wrong. Maybe a sixteen-year-old knows better."

Her father finally found his voice. "Come now, what do the blessed writings say? 'Together we thrive, alone we perish.'"

Thema ignored him. "No more nonsense, Afia. Is this what I raised you for?"

Afia closed her eyes. "Nonsense" was the word that her mother used to describe anything she didn't care to understand. And now that her own desires had been decreed nonsense, it was hopeless to argue.

"I'll do it," said Afia, without looking up. "I'll go through with the ceremony."

Her mother laughed. "As if you had a choice. Nobody skips their ewende. These young people . . ." She cast an exasperated glance at Nana Musu. "Do you think in my day I would have suggested such a thing? Mother would have buried me herself."

Nana Musu and Thema laughed, as though they were talking about someone else's hypothetical demise. Afia did not find this funny. She had been a fool to think that her mother would let her decide her own future, but it hurt to see her make fun of it.

Afia avoided her sister's gaze, dreading the confusion and betrayal that she knew she'd find there. Her father had resumed conversation as though nothing had happened. And her mother had already started using her favorite form of punishment—treating Afia as though she were invisible. Thema's eyes never landed on hers, and she made sure to address everyone else by name, to make it abundantly clear that her ungrateful child was not included.

Afia fought her desire to leave the table. She had thought that telling the truth would change what had already been decided, or at least make her feel better. But nothing had changed. Starting tomorrow, her life as a child would be over. There would be no more daydreams, no more excuses, only crystals and the start of a life she had never wanted.

4

THE QUARREL

That night in their room, the sisters prepared for the ceremony. Aya had picked out one of her silk wrappers and offered it to Afia wordlessly before sitting down to finish beading her ceremonial belt.

Afia longed to know her sister's thoughts but was too terrified to ask. Their room had always been their sanctuary from the outside world. On most nights, the sisters took turns braiding each other's hair, talking about everything that had happened that day. It was Afia's favorite part of the day, because they would tell each other all the things they couldn't say to anyone else.

Afia hoped that the book she got from the market would help to distract her from the silence. But as she reached for it in her bag, the gazelle figure tumbled out onto the floor between them.

"You still have that?" Aya said angrily. "Is that what you're planning? To run off with a stranger?"

"I—I wasn't," Afia stammered. "I'm not!"

"You *are*! Don't you know you were probably the hundredth girl he asked today?"

Afia's face grew hot with mortification. She had expected a bad reaction from Aya, but she had never seen her this angry before. "I broke one of his sculptures. I couldn't just leave."

"You wouldn't have broken anything if you hadn't stopped there. Why did he want you to meet him tonight, anyway?"

Afia hesitated. "He offered to take me to see the animals that he made carvings of."

"He wanted you to *leave* Dafra? Don't you remember what happened to Amadi?"

Afia's throat went dry. How could she not? The jali

often sang about the only man who had dared to leave Dafra. It had been ten years since Amadi, a mild-mannered tailor, had disappeared, his wife, Ilo, insisting that he had been lured away by a forest spirit. After a few days, Amadi had appeared outside the town gates, screaming and pleading to be let back in. His white robes were in tatters, and cuts and scrapes laced his arms. His eyes were wide, and he had kept glancing over his shoulder, as though some invisible terror were at his back.

Afia's mother had explained that the guards couldn't risk letting him in because there was no way to know whether that was truly Amadi or a spirit who had taken over his body. Afia remembered Ilo's expressionless eyes as she'd watched her husband pound on the gate. A group of children had greeted Amadi's cries with jeers and a shower of pebbles as the guards leveled their arrows at him. Afia was still haunted by his anguished cries when he'd realized he would not be allowed back in. He was never seen again.

"But, Aya," Afia said now, "you would know if it was me or a spirit. Wouldn't you?"

"Of all things, *this* is what you ask me?" Aya cried. "Tomorrow is the most important day of our lives, Afia. I thought we wanted the same thing."

Afia suddenly felt selfish. The thought of ruining her sister's initiation filled her with shame. "I won't leave," Afia said, putting her arms around her sister. "I promise."

Aya softened and squeezed Afia's hand. Afia knew that she had been forgiven, but she still felt uneasy. She had lied to her sister, and she had lied to herself too.

A smile brightened Aya's face. She held out a neatly folded square of cloth. "I got something for you."

Afia carefully unfolded the fabric. A delicate bracelet of amber beads shimmered in shades of yellow and orange. "Aya, no!" she cried. "How much was this?"

"Never mind. Do you like it?"

"It's beautiful," Afia said, slipping it onto her wrist.

"It's for protection and luck. There's no such thing as too much of either."

Afia frowned. She was already protected from the dangers of the outside world, even from the dangers of her own thoughts. Dafra made sure of that. Her parents made doubly sure of it. But her sister too?

Afia mumbled a thank-you. As she listened to Aya talk excitedly about the coming day, Afia felt a mixture of sadness and relief. She wanted more for herself, but if her sister was happy here, then what did it matter? Perhaps she needed to learn to find happiness here too.

That night, as they always did, the people of Dafra, young and old, shuddered at the sounds coming from the rainforest above the cliffs. Some covered their ears with blankets, others sang lullabies to their children, others cowered and trembled. Even though Dafra forbade its citizens from venturing into the forest, it could not keep the wild nocturnal sounds from creeping in.

But Afia lay awake, secretly delighting in the eerie noises. All her life, she and the other Dafran children had been told frightening stories of the forest.

"There are two worlds," Master Fọlámí always said. "The world of humans, and the world of the spirits. The forest is the domain of the spirits, and we have no business there. To set foot in there is to surrender to their whims. Even the strongest and most clever are powerless against them."

Afia remembered the time she'd found a dead butterfly, covered with ants. She couldn't take her eyes off the swarm slowly devouring the once-beautiful creature. What would it look like when the ants were finished, she had wondered. But her sister had dragged her away and said she was creepy for watching.

Afia felt drawn in a similar way to the forest. She knew it was dangerous and that she most certainly wasn't immune to the power of the spirit world. But she wanted to experience the dread and wonder of being there herself.

She thought of the caravan boy again, of how he had looked at her. She wondered if he had waited for her after all. She imagined him packing his beautiful animal carvings, looking up every now and then for a sign of the girl who would never come.

But as she watched her sister's dreaming face, Afia knew that she had made the right decision. And with that comforting thought, she was soon asleep.

5

THE GAZELLE

The morning passed in a blur. The sisters dressed and adorned each other's hair, arms, and necks with beaded jewelry and crystals. They fastened their ceremonial belts and wore anklets covered in painted bells that rattled as they moved. Aya barely spoke, which made Afia feel even more nervous. Their mother was also quiet as she helped their father and Nana Musu prepare the dishes for the ceremony.

On the street, the sisters joined the colorful line of sixteen-year-olds, trailed by their families dressed in their usual white. No one spoke, and the only sounds were of shuffling sandals and bells.

When they reached the town square, the elders sat in a straight row, crowned with crystals. A sumptuous feast was spread before them, brimming with every Djiombian delicacy imaginable. Crystals of every shape and size adorned the square, and the roaring fire in the center mirrored the dawning sun overhead. The whole of Dafra was in attendance.

Suddenly, the jali and drummers broke into song as a masked dancer, dressed head to foot in raffia, emerged from the shadows and began dancing. Afia felt sick with dread. The dancer was their mediator with the spirit world. Her ancestors were watching.

The elders rose. Aya turned back to look at Afia and squeezed her hand. The sixteen-year-olds stood together and recited a prayer, begging for guidance, and then began their dance. The masked figure whirled and stomped, indicating that their invocation had been received by the spirit world. The onlookers erupted into cheers.

The moment of their initiation had arrived. The elders began to shave each boy's head and cut off each girl's braids and topknot. They then traced a line of white chalk from forehead to chin on each of their faces to mark them as adults. Afia watched as the column shortened ahead of her. The newly initiated adults crossed the square beyond the fire, to their waiting parents and their new lives.

Suddenly, it was Aya's turn. Afia watched as the elder cut the braids that she had styled for Aya that morning, and as he dragged a white-tipped finger down the middle of her sister's face. She saw the proud smiles of her parents and grandmother as they presented Aya with her crystal comb. Aya gazed back at her—she had never looked happier.

The elder was shouting at Afia to step forward. Her hands grew cold. She wondered how many of the others in line behind her shared her dread, or if she was the only one who hesitated. She looked into the elder's face and recognized her instructor, Master Fọlámí.

"I'm proud of you, Afia," he said, readying his knife.

Afia didn't know what to say. She didn't feel that she had earned his pride or her mother's, or anyone else's. As he gripped the knot of hair at the top of her head, she gazed past him into the crowd.

To her shock, there stood the young man from the caravan, watching her.

He was impossible to miss among the onlookers clad in white, yet no one seemed to notice him. All the sounds of clapping and singing and drumming were drowned out by the hammering of her heart.

He had come back for her.

The young man smiled and turned away, disappearing into the crowd. Afia wrenched herself free just as Master Fọlámí's knife slashed. A gasp rippled through the crowd as Afia ran after the young man. She could barely see him ahead of her in the glare of golden light. The singing and drumming had stopped, and there came a volley of shouts and cries of outrage. She thought she heard her mother's voice, and Aya's. She was shaming her family and her ancestors. She was going against everything that she had been taught. But she ran on, not daring to look back.

Afia reached the north gate and was surprised to find it open. She paused. Beyond lay the forest that she had been warned away from all her life, but she closed her eyes and rushed through. When she looked up, the rainforest loomed before her, ominous and majestic in the morning mist.

She looked around, but the young man was not there. Had she lost him? Had she really seen him at all? Had she thrown her whole life away chasing a vision of her delirious mind? She began to hurl her ewende jewelry to the ground in frustration.

"Afia!" It was Aya's voice.

Afia froze. Her sister was not supposed to be there. Aya was not supposed to risk her own future for *her*. Afia turned, dreading another confrontation.

Her sister no longer looked like her. Aya's hair had been trimmed short, and the streak of white chalk seemed to split Aya's face in two. Her face was flushed with anger, reminding Afia of their mother.

"Do you realize what you've done?" Aya cried. "You need to come back immediately. I'll talk to the elders, and tell them you were—"

A look of horror came over Aya's face then, her eyes fixed on something behind Afia. Afia spun around. There at the edge of the forest stood the most beautiful creature she had ever seen—a white gazelle with a rust-brown throat and deep black eyes. The gazelle watched them solemnly.

"Afia, don't!" Aya warned.

But something about the creature's eyes drew Afia closer. To her surprise, it spoke to her. "I told you I would show you wonders. Here is the first one."

The gazelle's body was suddenly enveloped in white light, bending and twisting like hot iron. When the light faded away, there stood the young man from the caravan, his travel-worn tunic fluttering in the morning breeze. His large gold earring seemed to wink at her. She'd known there had been something otherworldly about him from the moment she had met him.

Aya uttered a prayer to ward off spirits and reached for Afia's hand. "I knew that young man was dangerous," she said.

But Afia was not listening. "I thought you had left," she said to the young man. "I thought I had missed my chance."

He smiled. "Selling shiny rocks for a living is not how I pictured you either. It takes courage to seek the path that is closed off to you."

Afia's heart leaped. He understood her. He had recognized and embraced her hidden dream, even before her own sister had.

"Afia, you promised you would stay," Aya protested.

The young man began walking toward the forest. "Say your goodbyes, Afia, but don't be long."

As he disappeared into the trees, Afia started after him. But Aya's voice stopped her.

"He's a shape-shifter, Afia. You know the stories as well as I do—"

"Yes, and they're just stories!" Afia snapped. "None

of you have ever set foot outside of Dafra. I'm tired of people who don't even know what's out there telling me how to live my life."

Aya fell silent. When she spoke again, she sounded dazed. "I don't understand. I thought you were happy. I thought we would always be together." Then Aya did something that Afia couldn't remember her ever doing. She began to cry.

Aya was supposed to be the stronger one, the one who could stand up to anyone. The one who could do anything. Afia wanted to hold her, to tell her that she would be all right. But she knew that if she did, she wouldn't be able to let go again.

"I can't stay," Afia said. "This is my only chance . . ." She reached for her sister's hand, but Aya backed away.

"You've made your choice, then. You've chosen yourself, instead of us."

A great chasm seemed to stretch between them, and for the first time Afia felt like a stranger in her sister's eyes.

"I'm sorry," Afia whispered. She stumbled away and ran toward the forest. When she glanced back, her sister looked tiny against the towering Dafran cliffs. She had a sudden longing to see her family one

last time. But she knew that they would never for-give her. As the forest closed around her, Afia surrendered to the rising wave of guilt and grief, and she wept.

6

IJÁBÙ, THE LAND OF WONDERS

Afia felt hollow, like one of the young man's carvings that was missing its amber piece. She wiped her face, unable to cry anymore, and looked around her. So this was the forest—the fabled land of the spirits. She held her breath, waiting for a host of spirits to descend upon her. But nothing happened.

She looked around, awestruck. Everything was *green*—shades of emerald, yellow-green, and deep viridian. It was the color of life itself, and she had never seen so much of it.

A twig snapped and Afia turned to see the young man

emerging from the foliage. His eyes moved over her ceremonial clothes before coming to rest on her face. "You were brave to take this step," he said. "But you don't have to do the rest alone." He offered his hand.

Afia thought of her family, her home, and everything she'd lost. She could never go back now, but his words filled her with hope. She took his hand. It was calloused and strong.

The ground was moist and cool beneath her feet now, unlike the stone streets of Dafra. The smell of trees and earth blended together. The farther they walked, the more shaded the forest floor became. Enormous trees soared into a deep green canopy that obscured the sky. The wind whispered somewhere high above, and the trees murmured back, creaking their ancient branches.

Above their heads, brilliantly feathered birds darted in and out of the trees. And there was a sound she had never heard before. It was a buzzing, a humming—the sound of every tree, every plant, every hidden creature pulsing with life. It was like listening to the chaotic

rhythm of millions of heartbeats and movements. Dafra was so quiet by comparison. To think that Aya would never see these sights . . . and if it weren't for the young man from the caravan, Afia wouldn't have either.

"I want to live here!" Afia shouted.

The young man laughed. "Wait until you've seen the palace."

Afia's eyes widened. "There's a palace?" Afia had heard of great palaces across Djiombé, but she never thought she would ever get to see one.

"It's a day's journey from here. I have a feeling that you and the Queen will enjoy each other's company."

"I've never met a Queen! What's she like?"

The young man smiled. "You'll see."

Afia's mind went in a hundred directions, trying to envision a queen in all her grandeur. Would she dress in gold, her face covered with a beaded veil, as Kadiri the Navigator had described Djiombian royalty? She was certain that any queen would have no shortage of interesting stories, at least.

After walking for a while, they stopped before a huge overturned tree. Its twisted roots splayed upward like a magnificent crown, and a gnarled doorway had been cut into the center of its ancient trunk. Afia peered through, but a thick curtain of mist obscured the view to the other side.

The young man was watching her with an unreadable expression. He removed one of the many necklaces he wore and put it around her neck. She recognized it as a talisman.

"What's in there?" she asked him.

He grinned. "Don't you want to find out for yourself?"

Of course she did. That was why she had left Dafra. Her trust in this young man surprised her. She had left home with someone whose name she didn't even know. Her mother would be furious, her father aghast. And she already knew what Aya thought.

"I don't know your name," she said awkwardly.

"Bakame," the young man said. "Tell me, do you know more about me now that you have my name?"

He fixed his dark eyes on her. There was a bold sincerity there. "You didn't need to know my name to know exactly what you wanted. That's what I liked about you from the start. You would've left home, with or without me. Because it's in your nature."

No one in Dafra had ever talked to her this way. Afia wanted to become the person that he thought she was, before he could find out that he was wrong about her.

"Well, if we get separated, at least I'll know how to call you," Afia remarked.

"We won't get separated." Bakame smiled. "Now follow me."

To her bewilderment, he stepped through the hole in the tree and vanished. She peered after him, but the mist on the other side was too dense.

Afia gazed behind her one last time. The forest seemed to stretch endlessly, and somewhere beyond lay the only home she had ever known and the people she loved.

Afia held her breath and stepped through the tree.

Her body felt strange, as if she was simultaneously being pushed, pulled, and twisted. But as the mist parted, there stood Bakame, waiting patiently for her.

"Welcome to Ijábù, the land of wonders," he said, taking her hand.

Afia looked around. These trees were ancient, with gnarled and tangled branches. The forest on this side was so dark that she couldn't believe it was still midmorning. Somehow she was certain that this was not Djiombé—this was some other land, or some other world even, far from anything she'd known.

"Where are we?" asked Afia.

"You have nothing to fear," Bakame said.

As they continued on, Afia heard the sounds of whirring insects and strange birdcalls, but there weren't any animals to be seen. When she mentioned this to Bakame, he nodded.

"You are new to this place. It would take days of

living here before your outsider scent is masked by that of the forest."

"I thought you were taking me to see the animals from your carvings," Afia said, unable to hide her disappointment.

"I am," Bakame said. "But I didn't carve them here. Patience, my dear girl."

Something about his manner made her feel more at ease than she ever had in Dafra, and her worries seemed to vanish with his words.

The deeper they went, the stranger the sights around them became. Trees grew out of other trees. Curtains of strange flowers dangled from branches. The canopy grew denser as they walked, and Afia struggled to avoid tripping over the roots that stretched across the forest floor.

"Can you imagine the weight of such a tree?" Bakame said, pointing to one of the enormous trees in front of them. "Those roots alone must support it."

At this, Afia grew even more awed of the trees, and of Bakame's knowledge. She doubted even Master Fọlámí knew as much. And Bakame was an adept forager too. As they traveled, he would slip away for an instant before returning with ripe fruit or mushrooms. From the hollows of trees, he would retrieve the clearest water Afia had ever tasted. He made fires just as easily and carved branches into skewers with a few skillful strokes.

Afia marveled as Bakame built a fire for their midday meal. "How did you learn all of this?"

"Surely you've made a fire before," he said without looking up.

Afia didn't answer. Her sister had taken it upon herself to learn how to run a household by watching their mother and Nana Musu cook meals. Afia had abandoned this after her mother had banished her from the kitchen for nearly setting fire to it.

"No matter," Bakame said. "The Queen takes good care of her favorites. If you win her affection, you won't need such knowledge ever again."

Afia was suddenly nervous about meeting the Queen. Whenever she had wanted someone to remember her, she had always relied on her sister. It was difficult to forget two identical girls with identical smiles. Would she be interesting enough to win a queen's favor on her own?

She pushed this thought away, feeling ashamed. How could she think about using her sister to impress a queen? She thought about how Aya must be feeling and felt even more ashamed.

Bakame rose and put out the fire. "We should keep moving. It's best not to travel by night."

Afia got up and followed him, eager to distract herself. The idea of being in the forest at night had never frightened her, but there was something in Bakame's voice that compelled her to stay close as the trees closed in around them once more.

7

THE VOICE IN THE DARK

They traveled on until dusk, and Bakame motioned to a circle of trees where they would settle for the night. The forest had fallen silent, and the trees looked eerie against the fading light. The occasional howl of an unseen creature broke the silence. Bakame explained that this was merely the sound of daytime feeders nesting for the night. Even so, Afia could not help but wonder what creatures were instead waking from their slumber.

Afia helped gather large kilipi leaves and branches for a pair of shelters. But Bakame refused to let her help any further, insisting on building them himself. *Am I really that useless?* Afia thought gloomily.

Afia watched Bakame work for a while but soon grew bored. Small golden lights began to dance in the descending dusk—fireflies. Bakame had restrained her impulse to study each of the strange sights along their journey in his efforts to cover more ground before nightfall. But Afia could no longer contain her curiosity. She waited until he was busy lining the interior of one of the shelters with leaves before she slipped away after the glowing dots of light.

The fireflies proved uncatchable though, and before long, the forest grew too dark for her to see the way back. The leaves above her head began to rustle fiercely in the wind. The string of her talisman became tangled in the dense underbrush, pulling tightly against her neck. Afia unfastened it and tried to free the talisman from the sharp bushes.

As her sight adjusted to the darkness, she thought she saw a face between the trees, or was it two? But when she looked closer, she could not see them anymore.

"Another lost one," said a voice. Afia turned, expecting to find Bakame, but there was no one there. Hysterical laughter filled the air.

"Who's there?" she demanded.

The voice now spoke directly in her ear. "Mind if I help?"

Afia gasped and put up her hands, but the disembodied voice only laughed at her.

"How does it feel to be afraid?" the voice asked. "It's been so long. I can't quite remember."

"What do you want?" Afia strained to see.

"I should be asking *you* that. You're in my forest, after all," the voice said. Afia could almost hear the speaker smiling as it spoke.

"Are you some sort of deity?" she asked.

The voice laughed again, this time for a very long while.

"Some sort of shrub spirit, then?" Afia said irritably.

"How quickly I've fallen in your estimation," the voice said with feigned offense. "You are a sensitive one, aren't you?"

Whatever this entity was, it was certainly annoying. Afia turned to leave.

"Wait!" the voice said. "I'm here to offer guidance. Admonitions. A friendly warning . . ."

"What do you mean?"

"Not everything is what it seems in this place. Follow your instincts, for your eyes will deceive you here."

Before Afia could ask anything else, a hand settled on her shoulder. She jumped.

"It's me," said Bakame. He held a glowing ember wrapped in a large leaf.

"I heard a voice," Afia said nervously. "Could it have been a spirit? I didn't think they could talk."

Bakame narrowed his eyes. He removed another one of his talismans and put it around her neck. "Keep that on, and don't stray away again," he said.

Afia was surprised to see him so agitated. As he led her back to their camp, she stared into the branches overhead, hoping to catch a glimpse of a figure, or of anything at all. But there was only darkness.

Bakame's small fire soon came into view, and it cast a warm light over the leaf huts he had built. They sat together in silence, watching the flames.

"You're thinking about your sister," Bakame said. She did not know how long he had been watching her.

"No," Afia lied. She wasn't ready to talk about Aya yet.

"She should be happy for you." Bakame was quiet for a while, the firelight flickering in his eyes. "You can't dwell on the past. No matter what happens, you can

only move forward. Never backward." He rose. "You deserve some rest. Today was not easy for you, but you are handling it well."

His words filled Afia with pride. She wished her family could see how brave she was. Already, she had traveled farther into the forest than any Dafran had ever dared, aside from poor Amadi, perhaps.

As she drifted to sleep, her thoughts brimmed with visions of palaces and queens, and the wonders that she would soon see with her own eyes. For the first time in her life, Afia didn't know what the next day would bring. And that was the most thrilling part of all.

8

THE PALACE

Bakame woke Afia as the pale morning light began to peek through the trees. The forest was just as magical as it had been the day before, but Afia only had a moment to take it in before Bakame was rushing her out of her leaf shelter. He had already foraged a breakfast of fruit, which they ate as they walked, and he seemed slightly on edge, no longer keeping to their more relaxed pace from the previous day.

They came upon two roaring waterfalls that would have towered over the highest Dafran cliffs. Bakame took her hand and guided her along a moss-covered bridge that led into the falls. For a terrifying moment, Afia's feet slid on the slick stones, but Bakame's strong grip kept her upright as they continued onward.

"Are you all right?" he said.

Afia nodded.

They traveled until they reached a wall of dense vegetation covered with strange red flowers and thorns. The wall seemed to stretch endlessly in either direction, blocking their path. Afia leaned in for a closer look. The leaves and branches were so tightly woven that they seemed impenetrable.

"Careful," Bakame said. He drew out his knife and sliced the surface. To Afia's surprise, the wall eased apart like a curtain. As soon as they had passed, the foliage knit itself back together behind them. Afia stared at Bakame, who continued on as though the most ordinary thing in the world had just happened.

They moved through a labyrinth of these flowered hedges until they reached a large courtyard with enormous sculptures carved from obsidian. They passed by one of a cheetah chasing an antelope, the elegant shapes of their limbs overlapping mid-run. At the far end of the courtyard stood a magnificent sprawling building. Countless tiny windows dotted its facade, and the carved sandstone walls reminded Afia of some of Kadiri the Navigator's drawings. Golden statues of a noble-faced queen lined the exterior, casting long shadows over them as they approached.

"Behold, Queen Ukiwa's palace," Bakame said.

Afia looked around in awe. If she had known that a Queen lived in a rainforest palace only a day's journey from home, she would have run away years ago. How she wished that her family could be here to see this. Especially Aya. If she saw this place, she would understand why Afia had *had* to leave.

As they ascended the grand stone steps leading into the palace, ironclad guards blocked their path. They parted as soon as they saw Bakame. Afia gazed at him in surprise, but he only smiled at her.

Bakame led Afia down a long hallway and into the throne room. "Wait here," Bakame said, gently releasing her hand. Afia realized with embarrassment that she had not let go of his hand since they had crossed the waterfall. He reached over and carefully removed his talisman from around her neck. "You won't need this here." He smiled. But as he strode away toward the throne, Afia wondered why he was still wearing his.

The ceiling soared over her head. Lining the walls were massive stone columns next to elegant wooden pillars carved with intricate human and animal shapes. High up on the walls, painted murals depicted a triumphant queen surrounded by kneeling admirers who offered their tributes. The longest rug that Afia had ever seen shone with flecks of golden thread and stretched before her across the polished stone floor.

Beams of sunlight poured through long narrow windows, but few reached the throne at the far end of the room. Stern-faced guards and richly dressed courtiers surrounded the throne. Many of them were Djiombian, but the rest were foreign to Afia, from lands beyond the sea.

Afia watched as Bakame leaned forward, appearing to speak into the darkness. One of the courtiers held a large umbrella over the throne, casting it in a deeper shadow. A jeweled hand caught the light, flicking an elegant fly whisk every now and then, even though there were no flies to be seen.

Bakame motioned for Afia to approach. He returned to Afia's side as she reached the throne. "This is Queen Ukiwa of Ijábù," he whispered. "Follow my lead." He took a handful of sand from a bronze vase before the throne and dropped to his knees. Then he prostrated himself and cast the sand over his head.

Afia did the same, though less gracefully. Her cheeks burned against the cold stone floor.

"You may rise," a guard's voice rang out.

Bakame took Afia's hand and gently pulled her to her feet.

Afia's eyes moved over the Queen's magnificent gown, made of hundreds of the strange red flowers that Afia had seen outside the palace, then to the gold jewelry that glittered at the Queen's wrists, arms, and throat.

"Do not look at the Queen unless she addresses you," Bakame warned.

Afia dropped her gaze to the floor, mortified.

A man in bloodred robes stood to the Queen's left. He regarded Afia with disapproval. "Quite the curious one, isn't she?" he said. A few courtiers tittered, but the rest remained silent, as if he had not spoken at all.

"King Ekwe," Bakame whispered to Afia. He gave a stately bow to the King before turning back to the Queen. "My Queen, may I present to you Afia of Dafra. She has journeyed bravely to make your acquaintance."

Afia kept her eyes on the floor. She didn't feel brave at all, but she didn't dare correct him. There was nothing about her that could possibly impress a queen.

The Queen's silvery laugh rang through the hall. "There is no need to avert your eyes, my dear," she said. "Any friend of Bakame's is a friend of mine. Come."

Afia stepped forward, but kept her eyes on the hem of the Queen's gown. Her father had told her stories about kings and queens when she was growing up. Her mother had said that looking upon their faces was like staring into the sun.

"What's the matter, dear? Am I that frightful to look upon?" the Queen asked. Her voice was warm.

Afia slowly lifted her head and found that she couldn't take her eyes off the Queen. She wore a beaded veil, parted to reveal a beautiful face. Her skin was obsidian smooth, and a delicate pattern of raised scars ran along each of her perfect cheekbones.

The Queen laughed, but not unkindly. She held out her hand. "Let me get a closer look at you, dear."

Afia glanced at Bakame, who nodded.

"You remind me of someone . . ." The Queen searched Afia's face. "Perhaps we've met?"

For a moment, Afia thought of mentioning that she had a twin sister but decided not to. "No, my Queen," she answered. "I would certainly remember if we had."

The Queen smiled and took Afia's hand. "Bakame says that you are an explorer, but allow me to make you another offer: Stay here as my guest, at least for one night."

Afia didn't know why she hesitated.

The Queen watched her. "You wound me, my dear,

by not saying yes right away. But I see that you are not like the others, who covet worldly things. I think I have just the thing that might tempt you though. Come with me."

The Queen rose, still holding Afia's hand, and led her out of the great hall.

9

THE GARDEN

Afia felt as though she had stepped into one of her books. All around her, the calls of songbirds mingled with the soft murmurs of fountains and trickling streams. Enormous walls encircled the garden, covered with bushes of the same flower that decorated the Queen's gown. The ground was carpeted with their red petals.

"This is my sanctuary," the Queen said. "Everything you see here is the most beautiful of its kind from all over the world. Ever since I was a little girl, I longed for such a garden."

Afia found herself in awe. The Queen had gone further than even the great explorers who merely documented their travels—she had created her own world. And what taste the Queen had! Each of the plants and flowers had been arranged into kaleidoscopic patterns, flowing from one color to the next. A majestic fountain stood in the center of dozens of hedges that spiraled outward.

A sudden movement caught Afia's eye. A leopard stepped out of the bushes and moved toward them. Afia drew back, but the Queen strode forward to meet it. As she did, more animals began to emerge from the greenery around them—cheetahs, lions, elephants, zebras.

Afia watched in amazement as the Queen knelt to caress each one. "These poor creatures had nowhere to go when I found them," the Queen said, running her fingers along a lioness's cheek. "I care for them and attend to their every want. There's not a living soul that wouldn't appreciate that."

Afia sat beside the Queen and watched the beautiful

animals roam about the garden and play together, unconcerned by which was predator or prey. She marveled at the flamingo's shades of coral and white, at the exquisite patterns on fur and scales of leopard and crocodile, at the fierce eyes, beaks, and fangs all around her. She tried to commit every movement, every gesture, every detail to memory. If only Aya could see what she was seeing, feel what she was feeling.

"I recognize these creatures." Afia turned to the Queen. "Bakame's carvings. Is this where he made them?"

The Queen looked surprised. "I would imagine so." She took Afia's hand excitedly, pointing out a pair of elephants to her. "Can you tell which is from the forest and which is from the savannah?"

"I'm not sure, my Queen," Afia admitted.

The Queen pointed to the smaller elephant. "His stature and the angle of his tusks allow him to move through dense vegetation. See there? His reddish tone blurs with the green of his surroundings as he moves."

Before Afia could react, the Queen pointed out another creature, and another, describing each in equal detail. Afia had never met anyone who shared her curiosity for nature. Even Bakame had hurried her along, seemingly more interested in their destination than the wonderful sights and sounds of the forest.

"You know so much," Afia said. "Are you an explorer as well as a queen?"

The Queen smiled a little. "I have traveled to many places, but I never did find what I was looking for out there. Perhaps someday I will find it here." She took Afia's hand. "I was just like you once . . . alone, without anyone to care for me. I've learned how rare it is to find people who truly understand you. When you find them, don't ever let them go."

Her words struck a deep chord within Afia. She found herself longing to tell the Queen everything that had happened to her, and how much it meant to her to be seen for who she really was.

But at that moment, a servant approached and bowed, whispering something to the Queen.

"I'm afraid I must leave you," the Queen said, rising. "There will be a ball this evening. Until then, my garden is yours to explore." She gestured at the bushes surrounding the garden with a smile. "And do mind the roses."

As Afia watched the Queen go, she fought the urge to follow her. She wanted to bask in the warmth of her admiration, to gaze upon her beautiful face, and feel the Queen's hands on hers again.

Afia got to her feet and soon lost herself in the garden, wandering along its winding paths. She noticed several of the animals drinking from the fountain closest to her, each waiting its turn. She found this curious but charming. A white butterfly fluttered over her head. Afia followed it to the garden wall, which was covered with roses. They were beautiful, their petals curling into perfect red spirals. She reached for one, but paused, seeing a thorn. She touched it to feel how sharp it was, and watched with fascination as a drop of blood slowly formed on her fingertip.

"I see you've found the Queen's favorite flower."

Afia whirled around to find Bakame there, watching

her. “Where have you been?” she asked, surprised by how quickly she’d forgotten about him.

“I didn’t want to get in the way of a new friendship,” Bakame said, drawing closer. He took her hand, and pressed his thumb over her wound. It was a small gesture, but Afia’s face began to grow warm. She found herself admiring the elegance of his hands and the outline of his profile.

Bakame let go of her hand and held up one of the blooms. “It is said that the King gifted the Queen a single rose from a far-off land. You can see now what she has done with it.” He nodded at a pair of gardeners nearby, filling baskets with roses. “I’m told it’s difficult to keep them alive in this heat. But the Queen’s gowns

require fresh cuttings each day. Only the most perfect flowers are used."

Bakame turned to leave. "There's something I must attend to. But I'll be in the palace should you need anything."

"Thank you for bringing me here," Afia said quickly. "Will you be at the ball tonight?"

"Oh yes, the Queen's ball is not to be missed," he said as he turned to walk back toward the palace.

Afia almost begged him to stay. She wanted him to walk around the garden with her, to tell her about each of the animals and why he had carved them. But Bakame had disappeared beyond the trees, leaving Afia to wander the beautiful garden alone.

10

A VISITOR

Dusk was falling over the garden, and most of the animals had withdrawn. But Afia remained, still entranced by everything she saw.

Something rustled in the hedge behind her. Afia looked up. There, among the roses, sat a wooden mask carved into the shape of a wildcat's face. It had the widest grin that Afia had ever seen. She reached for it, but the mask disappeared. She got to her feet, only to see the strange mask again above another hedge. It seemed to float, somehow worn without a wearer.

"Impossible," said Afia.

"Quite a lot of strange things are possible in this place," said the mask.

"It can talk!"

"It?" said the mask, with mock contempt. "I'm a he, if you *must* know . . ."

"I'm terribly sorry," Afia said. "I only see a mask."

"I'm not exactly welcome here," the voice said. "I merely wanted to see how you were getting on in this so-called garden."

Now Afia recognized the voice. It was the same one that had taunted her in the forest the night before, when she'd wandered away from Bakame.

"Who are you, and why are you following me?" Afia frowned.

"I'm afraid I can't answer the first question. Not in this dreadful place, anyway. And I already answered the second . . ."

"Dreadful?" Afia laughed. "Have you seen this garden? And the palace?"

"Oh yes," the mask said thoughtfully. "I used to spend quite a lot of time here."

Before she could ask anything, the voice spoke again, this time from the rosebush behind her.

"Not everything is as it seems in this place. They call the Queen's kingdom Ijábù, the land of wonders. A deceptive name, if you ask me."

"What's deceptive about it? I've never seen so many wonders in one place."

"Ijábù is only a fitting name to those who aren't *really* seeing," said the mask.

"I can see just fine," Afia said, with growing irritation. "You're quite rude, you know."

"I get that a lot." The mask sighed. "I never *mean* to cause offense." The mask was silent for a moment. "I had hoped that you wouldn't end up here, but I fell for the same thing, so I can't really blame you . . ."

"I didn't fall for anything. And I don't know what I've done to make you so interested in my decisions. I'm perfectly happy here, so you can go on your way." Afia turned away and headed toward the palace.

"A web can be beautiful"—the voice spoke again, following her—"but it is a trap, nonetheless."

"I don't see a trap," Afia said.

"It wouldn't be a trap if you could see it."

Afia turned back angrily. "Have you ever been to Dafra?" she asked. "*That's* the sort of place you're talking about. The rules and expectations there are enough to stifle anyone."

"There are rules here too," the mask quipped. "Ask the Queen if you can visit the forest, for example. The answer may surprise you. Or perhaps you enjoy it when people order you about under the guise of helping you."

"That's enough," Afia snapped.

"Oh, that was the line, was it? And I suppose I've crossed it," the voice said in a deflated tone. "Well, there are many ways to leave this place, but only one I would recommend. So listen carefully: *At the root of the palace, you will find many doors. But only one is large enough for a queen's heart and a king's backbone.*"

Afia was about to demand the meaning of this nonsense, but the mask began to vanish, until all that was left was a faint grin. Then that too disappeared.

Afia stood there, not quite sure of what she had just seen. A servant girl approached her and bowed. "The Queen requests your presence at the ball."

"Of course," Afia said, quite eager to forget such an absurd conversation. But as she followed the servant girl to the palace, Afia glanced back. The wildcat mask was there once again among the rosebushes, grinning at her.

11

THE MASKED BALL

The servant girl hurried Afia up a flight of stairs and into an extravagant bedroom, where two other servants stood waiting behind a steaming bath. Afia looked down at herself and was mortified at the state of her clothing. She wondered why the Queen had never mentioned it.

The girls began to unbraid Afia's hair. Afia stared at herself in the mirror as her braids fell past her shoulders.

One of the girls caught Afia's gaze in the mirror. "Would you like us to cut your hair?"

Afia paused. It was strange to think that her sister's hair was short now, that for the first time, it was different from her own. And she liked that.

"Absolutely not," Afia said.

The other servants looked up from their work with interest.

The girl who had spoken gave a quick nod, looking embarrassed. She pushed a book over to Afia. It was filled with illustrations of hairstyles for every hair type and length. Afia had never seen anything like it. She stopped at a page with intricately braided styles and pointed to one. "Can you braid it like this?"

The servant girl nodded again and hurried Afia into the bath. They bathed her first, and as they began detangling, washing, and conditioning her hair, Afia noticed that the servants did things differently than she was used to. Back home, she and Aya used a shampoo made with black soap and plant oils, but the servants massaged a rich clay wash into her scalp. Aya always used a wide-toothed comb, but the servants instead used their fingers to gently detangle her hair. Afia nearly fell asleep beneath the soothing movements of their hands.

The servants helped Afia out of the bath and draped a robe around her. They squeezed the water out of her hair, and parted it in sections to let it dry. She and her sister used to spend all day washing and braiding each other's hair, talking and laughing about every little thing. But she did not know anything about these women and did not know what to talk with them about.

The moon was high in the sky when Afia's hair was finally dry enough to rebraid. When they finished, Afia saw her sister's face looking back at her. Afia frowned. Even with a different hairstyle, she still looked like her sister. She glanced away.

The servants dressed her in a strange gown with long sleeves and a trailing skirt. They brought out a large headdress made of white roses and began fastening it to Afia's head, covering her hair.

"The Queen requires it," one of the girls said, looking apologetic. Then she put a mask into Afia's hand.

"The Queen is not to see your face either. Keep it covered as soon as you enter the ballroom."

Afia found this odd, but perhaps it was merely a whim of the Queen. She held the mask and ran her hand over the beautiful cheekbones, wondering if Bakame had carved it. Afia was suddenly nervous about seeing him and the Queen at the ball.

The servants began rushing Afia out of the room. "Quickly now," they said, guiding her down the staircase.

Murmuring voices and the glow of candlelight spilled

out from a grand door at the other end of the hall. The servant girls left her and retreated into the shadows. The girl who had given her the mask turned back to look at Afia. Afia smiled at her, but the girl did not return the smile.

Afia moved toward the voices, suddenly aware of how uncomfortable her shoes were. Inside the ballroom, extravagantly dressed courtiers danced to music from instruments that she had never heard before. The dancers held one another at arm's length, moving around the room in stilted circles. It was the sort of dance one might devise if one didn't actually like dancing.

The dancers all stopped to face Afia, staring at her through their identical masks. Afia quickly covered her face with her own mask. The courtiers nodded and resumed their strange dancing.

The glow of hundreds of candles cast the room in a golden haze. The whirling women wore rose-covered headdresses that looked like floating bouquets. The men, in their dazzling robes, moved lightly like birds.

Afia wondered which of them was Bakame. But no one spoke to her or approached her, apart from the servants with trays who offered her food and drink. She longed to join the dancers, but everyone seemed to have a partner, and she couldn't bring herself to cut in.

Just then, someone swept her up into a dance. Afia thought it was Bakame, until she noticed the young man's pale hands.

"Pardon my insolence," he said merrily, "but I've never been to such a wonderful place as this!"

"Neither have I," Afia said, trying to hide her disappointment.

Even through his mask, the young man's eyes were full of life, and his laugh struck a dissonant chord against the silence of the other courtiers. Afia found his enthusiasm contagious. They wheeled around the room, chattering and laughing.

Afia was about to ask him his name, but he stopped dancing abruptly. The other courtiers had stopped too and faced the doors. The Queen entered, magnificently dressed and flanked by red-caped guards. The King was not with her, but she was trailed by a group of courtiers dressed in red. Afia noticed that neither they nor the Queen wore masks.

Everyone bowed as the Queen swept past. Afia caught sight of Bakame, also unmasked, among the Queen's retinue. She had never seen him so richly dressed and was stunned by how powerful he looked. His face was tilted toward a female courtier in whispered conversation, and he did not look at Afia as he passed.

She watched as the Queen singled out one dancer, and then another, lavishing each of them with compliments. The other dancers rushed to be the closest to the Queen, to be the next to bask in her attention.

Once the Queen was seated, the dancing resumed. Afia noticed that the courtiers who had arrived with the Queen did not join the others, but instead chatted among themselves. Her dancing partner had left for the banquet table. Afia looked for Bakame again but could not find him.

A servant approached Afia and escorted her to the

Queen, who sat at a tall table with high-backed chairs. The Queen smiled when she saw her, and gestured for Afia to lower her mask. "Sit, sit, my dear. Have you eaten? A drink, perhaps?" She patted a chair beside her and motioned to a nearby servant, who promptly set down two sparkling goblets of palm wine.

As Afia removed her mask, several of the courtiers paused to stare at her enviously.

"You must tell me everything you did today," the Queen said eagerly. "What did you see? I want to know everything."

Afia was certain that she would bore her, but she began to tell the Queen about her findings, about the strange plants she had seen and the beautiful patterns that she had noticed on the leopard in particular. The Queen's eyes shone as she listened to her. Under the warmth of the Queen's affection, Afia had never felt so important.

That was when her thoughts returned to Aya. *She* was Afia's best friend, not the Queen.

Afia set her goblet down.

The Queen's brow furrowed, and she took Afia's hand. "What is it, dear? Have I upset you?"

"No," Afia said. "It's just . . . I can't help but think of my sister. Of how I left her."

The Queen listened intently as Afia told her about Aya, about how they had grown up together and had been each other's best friend all their lives. How she had hidden her own dreams in order to stay with Aya out of fear of breaking their bond.

"Then why did you leave her?" the Queen asked. "What did she do to offend you?"

"She didn't offend me," Afia said quickly. "I would have taken her with me, but she was happy in Dafra." She paused. "I never thought I could leave her. I intend to go back someday and tell her about everything I've seen. Maybe then she'll understand. Maybe then she'll come with me."

The Queen smiled, but the smile did not reach her eyes. "I know who it is that you remind me of," the Queen said. "My own beloved sister, Uzuri. She made me the same promise many years ago."

Afia was startled that the Queen would share something so intimate with her. She could see that the Queen was trembling.

The Queen appeared to be about to speak when a pair of courtiers in red approached her and bowed.

The Queen rose with an apologetic smile. "Enjoy yourself and forget your sorrows for tonight, my dear." She squeezed Afia's hand again and disappeared with the courtiers into the crowd.

The rest of the night passed like the dancers whirling before her. Afia saw Bakame leave with a group of laughing courtiers, but she did not follow them. She couldn't stop turning the Queen's words over in her head or wondering what the Queen's sister had been like. Surely, they had reconciled by now, as she and Aya someday would. Afia took another sip from her goblet and let the dancing and the music push her thoughts away.

12

THE KING

The Queen invited Afia to sumptuous parties each night but never returned to the subject of Uzuri, her sister. This perplexed Afia at first. But she was soon distracted by her desire to explore the many rooms of the palace.

There was an enormous library that reminded her of the stories about the great cities in the north, where scholars were said to journey from all over Djiombé. Afia had always imagined that such a library would be filled with scholars and their scribbling quills. But the

Queen's library was silent. Hundreds of books, manuscripts, scrolls, and even clay tablets sat untouched on the shelves and in piles on the floor, seemingly without any concern for their contents or origins. Afia decided to remedy this neglect and spent many hours there, reading everything she could about the animals she saw in the Queen's garden. She was surprised by how many of them came from lands that she had never heard of and wondered how the Queen had brought them all to her garden.

There were many other rooms that none of the courtiers seemed interested in—a room dedicated to all sorts of porcelain works, a room hung with hundreds of masks from every place imaginable, and a mirror room, filled with looking glasses of all sizes. Some were small enough to fit in her hand, others felt large enough to walk through. Some of the mirrors were old and dust covered, others were cracked, reflecting Afia's face in odd configurations.

As she moved through the palace, Afia noticed that the

courtiers spent most of their time in the lounges and dining rooms. The odd courtier could be found strolling about the balconies and courtyards, but strangely, the only people she saw in the garden were the gardeners and the occasional guard making their rounds. Afia hoped to run into the Queen again but couldn't find her in the garden or the palace.

Afia began to feel lonely again. As she wandered on, she came upon King Ekwe sitting alone in the throne room and approached him. Two stern-faced guards stopped her.

"It's all right," the King said, waving them away. He studied her for a moment, then frowned. "Be careful, young girl. Curiosity can be dangerous."

"My King?" Afia said.

"Loyalty is the most prized virtue of all here. Always remember that." The King gazed ahead, swinging his jeweled scepter in a lazy circle.

Afia considered asking what had prompted this rebuke, but he seemed to be the sort of person who was offended easily. "My King, I didn't see you at the ball last night. Or the night before."

The King's eyes clouded over, and Afia realized that she had managed to offend him anyway.

"My greatest joy in life is to be at the Queen's behest," he said. He sounded angry. "If she needs me, I go to her. If she doesn't, then I remain here."

"What happened to the Queen's sister?" Afia asked abruptly.

The King looked surprised.

"The Queen told me about how she left her," Afia continued quickly. "I just wanted to know . . . how it turned out."

The King pressed both hands to his scepter. "Uzuri." He spat the name as if it were repulsive. "She only cared about herself. Do you know, she threw away her sister's love for someone she barely knew? Uzuri fell in love with a boy and ran off with him. She never returned, never wrote to her sister. Ukiwa was only six."

The similarity of Uzuri's story to her own made Afia

regret her conversation with the Queen about how she had left Dafra. Had she angered the Queen, perhaps?

The King continued, "She still believes that her sister is out there, that she will hear about Ukiwa's magnificent garden. She thinks this will bring Uzuri back. Perhaps it will. But I've done everything to make her happy. Everything."

There was something frightening about the way the King said this.

"Sit, sit," the King chided. "Have you eaten yet?" He waved a servant over, who set down an attractive tray of small pies. They were the size of the meat pies that her mother made, but they had words stamped into the crust.

Afia hesitated.

"They're not poisoned," the King said in an irritated tone, biting into a pie with a bright purple filling.

Afia took one that read EAT ME and bit into it. It was far too sweet, but Afia quickly finished it, not wanting to offend the King again.

EAT ME

"Won't you sit?" the King said, gesturing to the floor. "Surely your parents taught you that it's rude to eat while standing?"

Afia bristled. The King was starting to remind her of her mother. "I'm sorry, my King"—she bowed—"but I must prepare for the Queen's ball tonight. Thank you for the pie." She turned to leave. When she looked back, she noticed how small the King looked, eating alone in the throne room.

Afia scoured the palace for the Queen. But the hallways and doors were beginning to look the same, and she was soon lost. No matter how hard she tried to forget the talking mask in the garden, Afia now found herself returning to his strange words. What did he mean by doors at the *root* of the palace? And what did it have to do with the King and Queen?

Afia stumbled into a room hung with red tapestries and curtains. She found dozens of courtiers lounging there. Some fanned themselves, others popped colorful confections into their mouths. They were a picture of elegant boredom. Cushions and pillows covered the floor, and the sweet scent of incense hung in the air. A strange fog began to fill Afia's mind, and she nearly tripped over several courtiers strewn languidly among the pillows.

"Watch where you're going," one of the women said. The courtiers around her giggled lethargically.

Afia muttered an apology and stepped around them.

A servant approached her, carrying a tray of small cakes and glass vials with words painted on them. Afia thanked him and took one with blue letters. DRINK ME, the vial insisted. Afia regretted it as soon as she took a sip—it was sickeningly sweet. She was beginning to wonder why the Queen was so fond of sugar.

"I remember you," a familiar voice said.

Afia looked down. It was her dancing partner from her first ball, lying on a pile of cushions. Without his mask, she could see that he was handsome, though not as striking as Bakame. He grinned at her, but his eyelids drooped as though he were half asleep.

Afia was about to introduce herself to him, but he interrupted her.

"The wonder of this place. And the Queen! She just gave me a private tour of her armory. I didn't have to tell her that I learned archery as a child—she sensed it somehow. She said that with some training, I could have a prominent place in her court. Can you imagine? The son of a farmer serving a queen!"

Afia felt a pang of jealousy. The young man continued talking, but each word came more slowly than the one before. As she listened, Afia found herself sinking into the cushions. She knew that there was something she had set out to do, but every time she came close to remembering, the thought seemed further and further away. All she wanted to do was lie there, basking in the softness of the pillows. The sunlight streaming through the windows felt like a gentle hand on her face.

Afia accepted a cake from a nearby servant's tray. It felt like she was taking a bite out of a small pink cloud. As her head drooped, she wondered why she hadn't seen Bakame today. Maybe he was hiding from her under the pile of cushions? She giggled and began to toss pillows aside, until she was turned away by two entwined courtiers whom she uncovered by accident.

Hours went by, and the waning sunlight played over her eyelids. Someone was tracing lines along her arm with delicate fingers. Afia lay there blissfully. Somewhere in the back of her mind, a voice was whispering about *doors* and *roots.* But Afia did not pay it any mind.

13

THE SECRET

When Afia awoke, she was in her bed. She didn't remember how she had gotten there, or why she had been tired enough to sleep until nighttime. Cursing herself, she propped herself up and noticed a sumptuous tea tray beside her bed. She wondered if the Queen had left it for her.

She took a sip of the tea, but it was too sweet. The dishes were sugary as well, and Afia found herself craving the peppery heat of her mother's fish stew. She thought of her family having dinner at home without her and wondered whether they missed her or hated her. She leaped out of bed and put on one of her ball gowns to distract herself. Not the most practical thing to explore the palace in, but she didn't care.

In the hallway outside her room, an odd stillness hovered in the air. As she made her way deeper into the palace, she heard a faint murmur of voices. She followed the sound to a pair of closed doors emitting a sliver of golden light along the bottom. She peered through the keyhole and saw that two guards were blocking the doors. Whatever was going on in there, Afia had no intention of missing it.

After circling the surrounding halls, Afia discovered a half-broken flight of stairs from which she could peer into the room through a narrow window. Inside, the courtiers stood in several neat rows. Their stately postures reminded her of her own ewende ceremony. The masks that covered their faces now had sharp skeletal features. Afia's eyes were drawn to a large candlelit shrine, decorated with what looked like skulls. What were the courtiers doing? Surely the Queen would never allow such a gathering.

Just then, the Queen herself entered. A row of skulls lined the hem of her rose-covered gown. A shiver ran through Afia as she stared at their grinning teeth. She could almost hear the horrible clattering of bone against the stone floor as the Queen moved to the center of the room. King Ekwe and a group of red-caped guards stood on either side of her.

A young servant stepped forward. She bowed and offered the Queen a bracelet from her arm. The Queen took it with a smile and held out a vial of red liquid to her.

The room fell silent as the young woman drained the vial. There was a flash of white light, like the one that had enveloped Bakame at the forest's edge, and where the young woman had stood only a moment before, there was now a zebra, pawing at the ground. Afia caught her breath. The columns of courtiers erupted in celebration, flailing and shouting.

The Queen waved her hand. The zebra returned to her human form, but she looked less lively than she had before, sickly even. Afia's thoughts flew to Bakame. She had never asked him where his ability to shape-shift had come from. Had he accepted a vial of red liquid from the Queen too? And did he expect her to do the same?

The guards brought a man forward next. Afia sat up, recognizing him as her dancing partner from the first ball. Now he appeared agitated. As soon as the vial was brought forth, he began to shake his head. The guards struggled to restrain him. The man shouted, and Afia barely caught the words "I won't!" and "I'll never!"

The Queen gave an inaudible command. Afia had never seen her look so frightening. A large figure wielding an axe stepped into view. The young man seemed to crumple inward, no longer the exuberant dancer that Afia remembered. The courtiers began to chant. Then the executioner's axe fell on the young man's neck. Blood spattered over the gold-encrusted walls and the polished stone floor.

Afia shut her eyes, but the image was still there.

When she opened her eyes again, the executioner was presenting the young man's head to the Queen. The Queen cradled it as though she were handling something precious.

Afia turned away and fled, feeling angry, feeling sick. She didn't even know the young man's name or what any of this was about. The words of the talking wildcat mask from the garden returned to her with thundering clarity: *Not everything is as it seems in this place.*

At last, she understood.

14

THE OFFER

Afia didn't stop running until she reached the empty garden. She now understood why there were no animals there at night, and why she had never seen any of the courtiers outside during the day. They were trapped in the bodies of animals in exchange for a place in the Queen's court. And if they refused her . . .

Afia fought away the image of her dancing partner's head in the hands of the person she had so admired. She wondered what the courtiers had thought of her, as she laughed and made conversation with their captor. The courtiers had all seemed so content, so carefree. Not a single one of them had tried to warn her.

But that strange talking mask in the garden had. Afia scoured the hedges now, determined to find its wearer and to beg him to show her the way out. But there, alone by the fountain, stood Bakame, drinking out of a goblet. The finery of his court regalia lent a harshness to his features that she had not noticed before. He was no longer the charming young man of the caravan, but the Queen's hunter, gathering her prey.

Bakame glanced up. "Unable to sleep?" he asked.

"You knew what this place was," Afia said angrily. "Were you planning this from the beginning?"

Bakame offered his goblet. "Go on. It'll take the edge off." Bottles of palm wine littered the ground around him. Several were already empty.

Afia ignored his gesture. "You're no carver. Who are you?"

"I *am* a carver. You saw my skill for yourself." He set the goblet down and held out his hands, turning them in the moonlight so she could see the callouses and scars. "But I am also the Queen's servant." He laughed a sad, mirthless laugh. "I carve now only when she allows me to."

Afia bristled. "Why didn't you tell me that you work for her?"

"You didn't ask."

"I left everything and everyone I loved behind. How could you do this to me?"

Bakame picked up his goblet and began swirling the wine, watching Afia from beneath heavy-lidded eyes. "The only ones who get beheaded are the obstinate ones. You'll be fine. Besides, she likes you."

"Take me back to Dafra," Afia demanded. "I'm not staying another moment with that murderer."

"Careful," Bakame said. "Others have been executed for less."

Afia knocked the goblet out of his hand and attempted to strike him, not caring that he was a shape-shifter, or that he had a knife, or that he clearly had the upper hand. She wanted him to feel pain. But he caught her by the wrist.

"That's expensive stuff to be feeding the Queen's plants with," he said calmly, pulling her closer. "You ought to thank me. Your head would have rotted with boredom in Dafra. You would have never experienced anything but a life of selling crystals for your mother."

Afia wrenched herself free. "I wish I *had* stayed there."

"But you're here now," Bakame said. "And the Queen will ensure that you live in splendor for the rest of your days. A fair trade, if you ask me."

"How many others have you brought here?" Afia glared up at him. "How many of them have been executed, or have you lost count by now? Look at you cowering here, drinking yourself numb while the people who trusted you are being killed."

Bakame's expression turned venomous. "I promised you wonders. And I delivered, didn't I? You never specified *how*, so you alone are to blame. There is a price to pay for everything in this world. Or did your parents never teach you that?"

Afia no longer recognized the young man who had seemed to care about her. She narrowed her eyes. "I deserved to know who this Queen was before you brought me here."

Bakame picked his goblet up and poured more wine

into it. "The Queen isn't hiding anything. None of us are. You simply failed to see it." He looked at her and sighed. "I had no choice. It is my job to bring new members to her court. If I don't, I'll lose my head. I was fooled just like you were. But I worked my way up to become the Queen's most trusted servant. I am the only one allowed to travel outside of Ijábù, and only I

can shape-shift at will, rather than at her behest. But you must understand. *Everything* has a price. That comfortable room of yours, the garden, these luxurious clothes. Did you really think your dreams would just be handed to you?"

Afia looked away. She couldn't let him see her mortification.

"Let me tell you a secret," Bakame said, putting an arm around her. "You need allies to get what you want in life. You're smart, Afia. If you listen and learn from me, we could truly be great together."

Together? A couple of days ago, Afia would have jumped at the chance to learn everything he knew, to travel the world by his side. She moved away from him. "If you're doing so well on your own, then why do you need me?"

"I don't." He shrugged. "I just hate to see wasted potential."

"I've had enough of your help," Afia said coldly.

Bakame watched her with an amused smile. "You fancy yourself an explorer. But I can see right through you, Afia. You don't enjoy hardship. You want to be taken care of. And everything you *really* want from the world is right here, without any of the discomfort or danger. Out there, nature is ugly. Even the trees and insects are your adversaries, and they've been at it for far longer than you."

"I left Dafra to see the world, to go wherever I please."

"Try having to travel for *years*, every day, with no end in sight," Bakame said severely. "The caravan used to be my life—walking through blistering heat and sandstorms just to sell my wares. Can you imagine the heels of your feet slowly grinding to bone?" He looked her over. "You wouldn't last a day."

"So you gave up?" Afia shot back.

Bakame laughed bitterly. "I gave up everything for that silly dream. My father taught me and my brother how to carve when we were little. My brother never had the patience for it. He wanted a carefree life. I joined the caravan to sell my carvings. But most of my time there was spent cooking for the others and feeding the camels, doing what I had to do to eat. To avoid being left behind.

"Forty markets a year—can you imagine how many people have seen my carvings? And I've only ever sold a handful. Most people would haggle ruthlessly, with little care for how much love I poured into my craft. Others would sweep by without even looking. I'll tell you, it's the *indifference* that makes you feel worthless. By the time I met Queen Ukiwa, there was nothing left of my dream. She offered me wealth and luxury that I could never hope to achieve by carving. And all I had to give her was my loyalty."

"But your sculptures are beautiful," Afia protested. "You gave up too quickly. You weren't in front of the right people . . ."

"That's what my brother said. He was foolish enough to believe that if you just follow your dreams, they will magically come true someday. But the world doesn't care about your dreams. So why not enjoy your time as well as you can?" He took another drink. "You shouldn't try to live off dreams, Afia, unless you mean to starve. I paid a steeper price than you know for that knowledge, and here I am, offering it to you freely.

Most of the people I bring here are fools, and to be honest, I thought you were one too. Here's your chance to prove me wrong."

That hit harder than anything else he had said to her. It was the sort of thing her mother would say. She found herself longing for her mother now, for her father and her grandmother. But most of all she longed for Aya.

"Think about it, at least," he continued as he bent to pick up the strewn bottles. "The Queen is no fool. If you do not truly love her, she will know. Here, I can protect you from her. But out there, I'm afraid you are on your own."

And with that, he strode off toward the palace, leaving Afia alone in the dark garden.

15

THE DOOR

Afia felt like she was falling. She had been so proud of herself for leaving Dafra, for making a decision on her own. Now all she felt was regret. She had left the people who loved her behind. She had hurt and shamed them in front of their entire community. All for a manipulative stranger who had told her what she wanted to hear, who made her feel more special than she actually was.

I have to get out of this place. Afia searched the garden, but she found no exits, and the rosebushes made climbing the walls impossible. She decided to try the palace gate that she and Bakame had entered through. She hurried into the palace, listening for approaching courtiers or guards. But before she reached the gate, she remembered that the courtyard in front of the palace was surrounded by a wall of roses. Without a knife like the one that Bakame had used, she would not be able to escape that way either.

Afia began to search the halls, peering out of each window. But at each window, the rose wall blocked her view to the outside. With mounting dread, Afia realized that the entire palace was surrounded by the rosebushes.

The grinning cat mask returned to her mind. He had said something about there being only one usable exit. Something about a door at *the root of the palace.* A cellar or dungeon, perhaps?

As she scoured the hallways, she came across a door that she didn't remember seeing before. It was older and much plainer than the others, and she wondered why she had missed it on her previous tours of the palace.

Afia opened it and found a stone stairwell covered with deep stains. She followed the winding steps down to a dark corridor lined with more doors. The air was cold and damp here, and the few hanging lanterns threw distorted shadows against the stone walls. There were strange sounds too—the scraping of metal against stone, a persistent knocking, and what sounded like a muffled cry.

Then she stopped. On the wall ahead of her hung a portrait of a young woman with high cheekbones. Her eyes stared at Afia with a hint of defiance. There was a small inscription on the frame: UZURI. Afia shivered as she recognized the face. This was the likeness carved into the masks that she and the others had worn at the ball. It belonged to the Queen's sister.

"A queen's heart," Afia whispered. That was it. *Only one door is large enough for a queen's heart and a king's backbone.* But which door was that?

Afia realized with some dismay that all the doors looked the same. She tried one door handle, then another, but they were both locked.

Just then, she heard the sound of shuffling feet and armor from the stairwell. Afia pulled on the nearest door handle, and to her relief, it opened. It was too dark to see anything, but the pungent odor of something rotting filled the room. She held her breath and peered out through the keyhole.

The King stepped into view, motioning impatiently to a guard holding a torch. Two other guards followed, carrying a shrouded corpse between them. It was headless. Afia looked away in revulsion.

When she peered out again, they were no longer there. Farther away, she could hear the King grumbling about something. Then came a heaving sound from one of the guards and the creaking of a door.

The hallway was silent once again. Afia waited a moment before venturing out. The King and his men had gone through one of the doors at the end of the hall, but which one? She tried each handle, but all of them were locked.

Afia was about to turn back when a glint of metal near the floor caught her attention. She knelt for a closer look. There at the bottom of the wall was the smallest doorknob on the smallest door that she had ever seen.

She smiled. *Only one door is large enough for a queen's heart and a king's backbone.* She should have guessed that the talking mask wasn't fond of royalty.

Afia knew how absurd this was, but she had to try.

She took the doorknob between her thumb and forefinger and pulled. An invisible force seemed to hold the door closed, but she pulled harder. With a loud groan, the door began to open and simultaneously grow in size, and when the door finally swung open, it was as high as the other doors. A string of wooden talismans hanging from the outer doorframe fluttered in the night air.

As soon as she stepped through, the door shut behind her and shrank back to its original size. Afia looked around, feeling relieved. She was not only outside the palace, but beyond the towering rose hedges too. The forest was only a short distance ahead, and she could just make out the guards digging beneath a stand of ìrókò trees. The King watched, holding a torch over them.

Afia waited to make sure no guards appeared along the parapets behind her. Then she crept along the tall grass between the rose hedge and the forest. By the time she reached the trees, the guards had cast their shovels aside and were lowering the headless corpse into the hole. She watched as the King began to move his hands in a trancelike state, murmuring words that she did not understand.

A spark of blue light rose out of the grave and vanished like a falling star. The King stood there for a moment, looking after it in silence. "Another life," he murmured. He motioned to the guards, who took up their shovels again. When they had finished, they started back toward the palace, leaving the ìrókò grove in darkness.

Afia approached the grave with her head bowed. She wondered where the young man's home had been before Ijábù and whether his family was still out there waiting for him. Before turning away, she picked up a small stone and set it carefully down on the grave.

But she couldn't stay here, so close to the palace. As she stared into the darkness, all the stories that she had grown up with about venturing into the forest alone at night came back to her with awful vividness.

There came a shout from behind her. One of the guards had his torch raised in her direction, signaling to the guards on the tower.

Afia plunged into the dark, just as the blare of a hunting horn reached her ears.

16

THE SONU

Afia ran. As she moved farther from the palace, the darkness seemed to swallow her completely. The air was heavy with an eerie presence, and she thought she heard voices whispering in the trees. She ran faster.

Afia cursed herself for being so gullible, for believing Bakame's lies. She had relied on Aya for everything back home, and on Bakame during their travels. If only the elders and her family had taught her how to survive, instead of spending so much time warning her against leaving Dafra. Now she would die alone, becoming another tale that her people would warn their children about.

There came a crashing through the foliage behind her. She glanced back. A white gazelle was closing in on her—Bakame. Afia's legs ached, but she willed herself to stay on her feet. She spied a river at the bottom of the steep slope ahead of her.

His voice stopped her as she reached the riverbank. "It's not too late."

Afia closed her eyes, struggling to catch her breath.

"The Queen doesn't know you've left her. If you come back now, you can take your place by her side without consequences. But once you cross that river, you will be beyond hope of forgiveness."

Afia faced him angrily. "Your words don't work on me anymore, Bakame. I know who the Queen is now."

He turned back to his human form and watched her, calculating. "It's a cold night, and you don't know your way. There's a warm bed still waiting for you at the palace. Come. We can talk more in the morning." He offered her his hand.

The thought of being alone in the forest at night frightened Afia so much that she hesitated for a moment. But only for a moment. She would never go back to that place.

Summoning what little confidence she had, Afia turned her back on Bakame and plunged into the river. The water was so cold that it nearly knocked the breath out of her. The current was strong, and Afia seized hold of a large branch to keep afloat. When she looked back, Bakame was still there on the riverbank, watching her. Then he and the looming palace, with its many glittering lights, were lost behind the dark tangle of trees.

Afia scrambled to the opposite bank as soon as the river slowed. The soaked and shredded fabric of what had once been her ball gown clung to her in the night air. She wrapped her arms around herself and trudged into the forest.

Afia looked up, searching for the stars that she had

grown up seeing above Dafra. That was how the explorers she had read about would navigate over land and sea. But the forest canopy obscured the night sky, and she could not tell which way was home.

She heard a strange call that sounded like a poor impression of a bird. "Who's there?" she called, trying to sound braver than she felt.

A two-legged creature with a large curved beak emerged from the darkness. Afia drew back, ready to run. But it was only a man wearing a carved hornbill mask. His body was covered with some sort of mantle made from feathers, branches, and leaves. He stood there, looking at her rather timidly.

More figures began to emerge from the trees. Each of them wore the same strange mantles, but their masks were of different birds—a spoonbill, an ibis, an eagle, even a guinea fowl.

The man in the hornbill mask began to remove his mantle, and Afia noticed that he wore a second one underneath.

"You must be cold," he said, draping the mantle over her shoulders.

Afia shivered her thanks. The mantle was scratchy and uncomfortable, but she felt warmer.

"We lost ones must look out for one another," the masked man said. "Do you have anywhere to stay?"

Afia did not answer.

"Come. We can take you to our shelter. It's not as fine as the palace, but you are welcome to spend the night."

Something about the man's forlorn manner made her relax a little. Afia nodded, relieved that she did not have to travel alone.

"What are your names?" she asked, trying to make conversation.

The man looked nervously at his companions, then back at her. "We are the Sonu," he said. "It is dangerous to reveal our names here, where there are eyes and ears all around."

Afia began to feel uneasy again. She noticed the others watching her and exchanging whispers.

"What did they serve at the palace tonight?" the one wearing an ibis mask asked her eagerly.

"Savor the memory of it," added another, wearing a spoonbill mask. "I wish I could still remember the taste of those sweet pies."

"Quiet," hissed the man with the hornbill mask. "You'll upset her." He turned to Afia and said in a gentle voice, "You will miss the palace for a while, but I promise that it's not so bad out here."

Afia wasn't sure what they were talking about. "I hope I *forget* everything about that horrible place," she told them.

The Sonu behind her began to mutter among themselves.

The man with the hornbill mask put a sympathetic hand on Afia's shoulder. "That's a natural response. But it wasn't your fault, you know. The Queen always kicks out the most interesting courtiers and keeps the most vapid ones. Being thrown out is a compliment, really, as difficult as it may be to accept."

Afia stopped and stared at him. "I wasn't kicked out. I escaped."

At this, the Sonu on either side of her sprang away. The man with the hornbill mask withdrew his arm from her shoulder.

Afia glanced around at them. "Did I say something wrong?"

"You left willingly?" asked the man in the hornbill mask.

Afia was perplexed. "Didn't you?"

A man wearing an eagle mask burst into tears, and the figures around him set about consoling him.

"This is unheard of," murmured one.

"Unprecedented!" cried another.

"What suffering we have endured, deprived of the Queen's exquisite care," wailed a third. "How patiently we all have waited for her invitation to return to her court. But you! You just *left*?"

"Please, I need your help. Bakame knows that I escaped and is probably on his way here now with the guards."

The masked figures began to flurry this way and that.

The man with the hornbill mask turned and spoke to Afia gravely. “Nobody has ever abandoned the Queen. If she were to catch us helping you, we would lose all hope of winning her favor again. I’m sorry, but we can’t risk that. Good luck to you.”

“Wait!” Afia pleaded. “I need to get home, and I don’t know the way.”

But it was no use. Many of the Sonu had already fled into the trees. The man who had given her the mantle now asked for it back. He seemed embarrassed, but Afia gave it to him and watched him disappear into the night with the rest of his companions. She turned away, feeling even more alone now.

The deeper Afia traveled through the forest, the more she felt like she was going in circles. The same trees, the same haunting sounds followed her, and it felt like there were eyes everywhere, everywhere. Ijábù was no longer the whimsical place that she had dreamed of from the comforts of her bed. She understood now why her people had dreaded the sounds of the forest for so many generations.

A white-blue light flickered. Then the forest shook, and a terrific rumble reverberated high above. Rain crashed down, erasing all semblance of a path. The forest floor began to turn into mud, but Afia struggled onward. Her skirt tore, entangling her legs. Pain shot through her knee as she stumbled on, soaked in sweat, rain, and mud.

Perhaps Bakame had been right and she had been a fool to throw away the comforts of the palace. Afia had blamed her parents for never teaching her survival skills, but what had she ever done to learn them on her own? To ask others how to survive?

No more dreams, no more foolishness, she told herself. If she survived this night, she would go straight home and beg her family to forgive her.

The rain stopped, and the forest fell into eerie silence. Afia found refuge between the sprawling roots of a tree and sank to the ground. Her knee pulsed with pain, and so did the cuts that showed through her tattered sleeves. She would be captured soon if she didn't fashion something more practical out of her gown. She set to work tearing the skirt and sleeves, grateful for her years of mending and repairing her own clothes to avoid her mother's reprimands. When Afia was finished, she smiled. Not even the Queen would recognize the dress now.

It was a small triumph, but Afia allowed herself to savor it before settling down to sleep. She thought again of her sister, alone in their room, and wondered if she was also awake. She ran her fingers over the smooth amber beads around her wrist. Aya had every right to hate her, to turn her away at Dafra's gates like Ilo had done with Amadi. But Afia had to see her again. She had to tell her how sorry she was, to try to repair what she had broken between them.

The last thing she remembered was the maddening whirring and clicking of insects all around her. The sounds of the night that had seemed so far away from her window in Dafra now filled her ears, until she surrendered to their relentless serenade.

17

THE BOY WITH THE CAT MASK

When Afia awoke, it was sometime before dawn, and the forest was cast in a pale gray haze. She sat up and peered around the side of the tree that she had fallen asleep against. There was the same grove of ìrókò trees from the night before, and the lights of the Queen's palace leered at her from beyond the branches. All the progress she had made the previous night, all that effort, utterly wasted. She might as well have curled up to sleep at the Queen's door. Had she lost her way, or was Ijábù itself playing tricks on her?

"Missing the Queen already?" said a gleeful voice from somewhere above her. "I *knew* you were mad."

Afia looked up. There, perched on a tree branch, was a lean-limbed boy, perhaps a few years younger than she was. He wore a grinning wildcat mask, and its pointed teeth gleamed in the morning light.

"You're the voice from the garden," she said, surprised.

The mask seemed to grin wider. The boy sprang to another branch, and Afia noticed that the mask was not fastened, but hovered in the air. His skin was painted with a pattern of white stars, which made him look like the night sky when he moved. He leaped from branch to branch with a dancer's grace, and his laughter rang through the trees.

"Be quiet!" Afia hissed. "The palace is right there."

But the boy ignored her. "We need to celebrate this momentous occasion. Nobody ever escapes the palace in one piece . . . but you are entirely whole!" He broke into more raucous laughter. "I suppose my riddle *did* work!"

This made Afia angry. “You knew that the Queen was beheading people? Why didn’t you speak plainly?”

“You wouldn’t have listened to me if I had.” The boy laughed. “I’ve tried everything to get people to leave that place. Scaring them doesn’t work. Waiting for them to figure it out doesn’t either. As soon as you tell people what to do, they’ll do the exact opposite because it wasn’t *their* idea. After watching so many people walk into the same trap . . . you have to find the humor in it, or you’ll go mad.”

Afia wanted to be angry, but he was annoyingly right. She must have sounded ridiculous defending the Queen. “Why did you sneak into the garden? Aren’t you afraid of her?”

The boy laughed. “The Queen can’t do anything to me anymore.” His body suddenly vanished, leaving the cat mask to bob and float in the pale light.

Afia leaped to her feet.

“Don’t leave,” the boy pleaded. “It’s quite lonely here, and you are the first living person I’ve talked to in a long while.”

"You're a ghost?"

"Would you like me more if I said I wasn't?" The mask looked rather sad in spite of its carved grin.

"No." Afia softened. "It's just that I've never met any sort of spirit before. My mother says that you steal souls away and inhabit the bodies of the living."

"Why would your soul be of any use to me?" The boy's body reappeared. "Mine is good enough."

Afia found herself suddenly more curious than afraid. "How did it happen, if you don't mind the question?" she said carefully.

"Oh, this?" The boy moved the mask away to reveal his severed neck.

Afia covered her mouth.

The boy let the mask drift back into place. "The Queen found me a little too tall, so she took a bit off the top." He laughed when he saw Afia's unimpressed look. "Actually, the Queen doesn't approve of questions. She prefers people whose heads are full of nonsense. It's a bit of a long story how I ended up here. You can call me Ojike."

"Pleasure to meet you," Afia said. "I'm—"

"Afia, I know," Ojike said eagerly. "I know each of the Queen's victims. I know which ones get beheaded and which ones are spineless enough to join her court instead."

"So, you didn't, I take it?"

"Certainly not!" Ojike drew himself up in mock offense. "I don't have enough self-loathing. And I'm not the only one."

"There are others?" Afia glanced around.

Ojike waved his hand. "Ijábù is *filled* with spirits. But few of them are as . . . dedicated as I am to helping the living." He said this with great pride.

Afia glanced at the base of the ìrókò tree where the guards had dug the grave, half expecting the beheaded courtier to join their conversation. But something else caught her eye. A row of spear tips glistening beyond the trees, heading in her direction.

"Guards!" Afia whispered. "They'll see us!"

Ojike shrugged. "They can't see *me*. The Queen

makes sure that anyone traveling through the forest wears talismans, to protect them from spirits. It's no use heckling them. They can't hear me either."

"But they can see and hear *me*," Afia whispered back.

"Then what are you still doing here? Come along," Ojike said, sailing away into the trees.

Afia suppressed her annoyance and rushed after him. She struggled to keep up, stumbling over outflung tree roots. Ojike's mask bobbed ahead of her, grinning.

When they were far enough from the palace, the boy stopped and turned to her eagerly. "There's something else I need to tell you."

"Well?" Afia said impatiently.

Ojike began to prance about with excitement. "I know how to break Ukiwa's spell," he said. "And you can help me do it."

The look that Afia gave him was reproachful enough, because he quit his capering. "Oh, you thought she was an ordinary queen who enjoys murdering and controlling people," he said. "I'm afraid she's more than that. She's a sorceress, you see. She made the shape-shifting potion. She collects people who wander into Ijábù from Djiombé and beyond."

Afia couldn't believe what she was hearing. Her mother and the elders had warned her all her life about sorcerers, but Afia had dismissed these stories as nonsense. Had they been right about this too?

"You'll soon meet some of the poor wretches who have been cast out from the palace," Ojike was saying. "They're called the Sonu, the lost dreamers. When the Queen loses interest in her courtiers, she leaves them to fend for themselves in the forest. But for some reason none of them has ever left Ijábù. There has to be a spell that binds them to the Queen, somehow. She knows that they can never truly escape her."

Afia frowned. Did this mean that she would have been trapped in Ijábù forever if she had taken the Queen's potion? But then why did the Queen need guards? "I've met the Sonu already," she said. "Have you asked them if they know of any spell?"

"I've tried, but they are so easily offended," Ojike grumbled. "One more thing—the Queen targets dreamers. They remind her of her sister. Quite creepy, if you ask me . . ."

"And what about the King?"

Ojike laughed. "That parasite? He cleans up after the Queen, not that she appreciates it. He was the one who thought of putting talismans over every door of the palace. But he doesn't have them in the garden, you know."

Afia hadn't thought much of it when Bakame had given her one of his talismans and certainly hadn't realized that she had only been able to hear Ojike's voice after she had taken the talisman off. As much as she hated to give him any credit, if it hadn't been for Ojike, she would undoubtedly be a shape-shifting courtier by now, or worse.

"I have to get out of here," she said suddenly, moving away from him.

Ojike jumped up. "Please don't go. I've been waiting to see the day that Ukiwa is overthrown. You're the only one who is not under her influence. Doesn't that make you want to stop her?"

"It makes me want nothing more to do with her," Afia said. "Besides, I don't know a thing about magic."

"You don't need to. I've searched every corner of Ijábù, and I *know*—well, I'm fairly certain—that Sékou holds the key. He is a shaman and guardian of the mushroom forest. But only you can persuade him to help us."

"Why don't *you* do it?" Afia said irritably.

"I have my limitations as a spirit," he said, sounding

a bit ashamed. "And in my efforts to learn more about the spell, I may have quarreled with everyone who could possibly help me. Including the shaman. Especially him."

Afia shook her head. "I can't help you. I have to go home and figure out how to face my family."

"Oh? Which way do you think home is?" he asked.

"I'll find it."

"How?"

Afia ignored him and kept walking.

Ojike's mask appeared beside her. "Just so you know,

you're going the wrong way. It's a big forest, quite impossible for an amateur. If you help me break the spell, I can show you. And you'll never have to see me again after that."

Afia paused. He was insufferable, but he was also right. She didn't have the slightest idea which way Dafra was.

"All right." She offered her hand reluctantly. "But you need to promise me that you'll speak plainly. No more riddles, do you understand?"

Ojike tossed his mask into the air with a celebratory laugh. "You have nothing to worry about." He took her hand eagerly in both of his.

She should have expected it, but it felt like she was grasping air, rather than flesh and bone. Afia hoped that she hadn't just made another terrible mistake.

18

THE GIRL & THE GHOST BOY

When Afia looked behind her, the forest looked stranger than it had just moments ago. And Ojike meandered back and forth as he led her along, in what seemed to Afia like a nonsensical manner. She began to wonder if he was doing this on purpose, to make sure that she could not figure out the way home. Or was this land itself nonsensical?

The branches seemed to twist into gnarled, predatory shapes, and Afia found herself rushing Ojike along.

"It's just earth and plants and trees," Ojike teased. "Nothing dangerous."

"It may not be dangerous to you," Afia said.

"Where's the girl who ran off into the dark, chasing fireflies?" Ojike complained. "Bring *her* back."

"That girl was naïve." Afia frowned. "But I know better now."

"You sound like the Sonu. They always insist that they know more than everyone else, when really, they are just more miserable."

They went on arguing, and soon came upon a carpet of fallen fruit with a flock of birds feasting on it. The birds scattered as they approached.

"Every morning, the monkeys and birds fight over their first meal," Ojike said, "so you can always find something that they missed down here."

Most of the fruit had been picked clean or trampled, but Afia hadn't eaten since the previous night. She picked up a bruised mango and devoured it.

Her feet were already tired, and Afia noticed that Ojike avoided walking, preferring instead to leap from tree to tree. She began to envy him, until she remembered why he could travel that way. He looked at her, as if he knew what she was thinking.

"What is it like being . . . ?"

"Dead?" Ojike perked up. "It's fantastic. Yes, I'm always cold and hungry, but I was cold and hungry before. Now I can heckle to my heart's delight. Besides, there are worse things."

"Worse than death?"

"Oh yes," Ojike said with great fervor. "Living under someone else's tyranny, for example. Rules aren't meant to be followed. Especially if they're ridiculous. I'd rather make up my own."

"I can see why you didn't get along at the palace," Afia said. "What about your family?"

"They disowned me." Ojike grinned. "They never approved of my ways. The last family I had was my brother, but we had a falling out too." He shrugged. "I don't hold any grudges. Family is more trouble than it's worth."

This horrified Afia. She told him how she had left

home because she had dreamed of seeing the world, but she realized now how wrong she had been to leave her family. How much she wanted to go back.

Ojike shrugged. "Your parents have already disowned you for leaving, and nobody would let you back in, anyway. What's the point in trying?"

The look that Afia gave him made Ojike shrink back.

"I didn't mean that," he said quickly. "I was talking about myself, not you. I'm told I do that a lot." When she did not answer, he added, "What I meant to say is, most people waste their whole lives searching for someone who will understand them. But you have yourself. Why do you need anyone else?"

"It's not that simple," Afia said. "I've never been without my sister before, and it just doesn't feel right."

Ojike's mask shifted to one side. "Sounds like you just have to get used to it. Life is too short to dwell on those who hurt you, unless you're going to do something about it. Like overthrowing a tyrant queen." He brightened. "You know who I'm dying to know more about? The Queen's stuck-up manservant. He wears more talismans than the rest, so I can never get to him."

"Bakame," Afia said sharply. "I should never have listened to him. I should have stayed home, like my sister."

Ojike laughed. "So after one bad experience, you're giving up on seeing the rest of the world? Remind me again how long you've been away from home?"

"Long enough," Afia said. "How long until we reach this mushroom forest of yours? And what do I do when we get there?"

"We'll feel it out as we go," Ojike said.

"We *are* going to see the shaman?"

"Yes, yes. Sékou, the truthsayer, the shaman, the guardian of the mushroom forest. Same difference. He's the oldest denizen of Ijábù. He knows everything."

"What did you do to upset him, anyway?"

Ojike let out a peal of laughter. "The shaman? I stole his pipe. He never forgave me for that. It was his favorite one too."

Afia shook her head and laughed too. She hoped the shaman had a sense of humor.

They had reached a cliff and Afia peered out over the edge. But the light from beyond the treetops was fainter now, and the ravine was cast in such deep shadows that Afia couldn't see the bottom.

"We should jump," Ojike said cheerfully. "It doesn't look that far, and those guards will never think to follow us."

Afia took a step backward. "You must be joking."

"You should be ashamed that a dead boy is more alive than you," Ojike teased. "I would gladly welcome the thrill of a harmless tumble down a hill. Come on, it'll be over before you know it."

"It might be harmless for you, but it won't be for me," Afia snapped.

Ojike soared up over the trees and looked around. "Well, no way across or around." His mask gleamed as he turned in the air above her. "Oh, and something is upsetting the birds and monkeys back there. Whatever it is, it's headed toward us." He returned to float beside her. "So, the options are . . . jump?"

Afia glared at him. She took a deep breath, but when she let it out, she was not any more relaxed.

Ojike laughed.

"I'm concentrating!" Afia said. She gathered her resolve into a breath and jumped into the darkness. As she imagined the rocks or thorns that would break her fall, she fought the urge to scream. But to her relief, she landed on a pile of dry leaves.

"You see? You *did* have it in you!" Ojike shouted. "Now, how did that feel?"

"Like I nearly joined you on the other side."

"Nothing like almost dying to make you feel alive. What you need is more unpredictability in your life."

"No," Afia said, getting up. "What I need is to go home. And you agreed to show me the way."

"We have a long way to go before that," Ojike said cheerfully. When Afia didn't respond, he lifted a finger. "May I offer a suggestion?"

"If you must," Afia said.

"You think too much. If you would just . . ." Ojike let out a loud exhale, ". . . let go, you would see things more clearly."

Afia heard something and motioned for Ojike to be quiet. Whatever had been following them was moving through the foliage much closer now.

"This way," Ojike whispered.

They hid behind a boulder just as the silhouette of a white gazelle came into view above them. Afia froze as the gazelle sniffed the air and looked out over the cliff. The gazelle stood there for a moment, seemingly confused. Afia could tell that Bakame was looking for her, but he paced back and forth, looking from the cliff to the trees behind him in an agitated manner.

He doesn't believe I could have jumped, Afia thought. She felt a surge of pride at her own bravery.

Bakame gave a frustrated toss of his head and disappeared into the trees.

"If only the Queen didn't put so many talismans on

him . . ." Ojike said, gliding back toward the cliff. "Do you think he'd notice if I stole a few?"

"Will you stop?" Afia whispered. "You're going to get us captured with your antics."

"I can be as loud as I like; they can't hear me, remember?"

"Is there anywhere we can hide?"

"Well, there is *one* out-of-the-way sort of place." Ojike grinned. "Are you fond of tea, by chance?"

19

THE TEA CEREMONY

Afia marveled at the underground tunnels that opened up before them. Giant tree roots wove and twisted together into ceilings and walls. Lanterns illuminated the path along cavernous hallways and rooms decorated with twisted liana vines.

"The Sonu can be a bit mad, but they are harmless," Ojike explained. "Since they cannot escape the forest, they have created their own world beneath it."

A pair of bird-masked people passed them, wearing cloaks made out of bits of forest.

"They disguise themselves when they're aboveground."

Ojike nodded after them. "There was once a band of Sonu who resisted the Queen. But that merry band was rounded up and either executed or left to rot in the palace dungeon. None of the Sonu have dared to interfere with the Queen since. So it's best not to mention your escape, or the spell, or any of it."

Ojike stopped in front of a large round door made from twisted roots. The tinkling of silver against glass and the sounds of laughter could be heard from within, and a rich aroma that reminded Afia of her mother's cooking wafted out. "There's someone here that you should meet," Ojike insisted. "Besides, we have a long journey ahead, and these folks will gladly feed you."

Afia felt that they didn't have time, but her stomach forced her to reconsider. "All right, but we leave immediately after."

"Good! One more thing," Ojike said. "Unfortunately, this is one of the many places where I am no longer welcome. But don't worry. I'll be at your side the entire time."

"You're not very good with people, are you?" Afia said as she watched him fade into nothing.

"Perhaps *they* are not very good with *me*. Did you ever consider that?"

Afia shook her head and pushed the door open. A dozen people clamored about on cushions and stools, chatting and laughing. The low table in the middle of the room was covered in all manner of kettles, teacups, and plates. Streams of daylight from the forest above and dozens of hanging lanterns lit the room, throwing shadows all around.

The pair of Sonu that had passed her and Ojike in the hall were removing their masks and sitting at the table to eat. A small child crawled about on the table, making a mess wherever he went. Three older children raced around the room, clattering sticks on the branches and roots that made up the walls. At the far end of the table stood a man and a woman loudly fussing over each guest, making sure that everyone had what they needed.

"Those are the hosts," Ojike whispered in her ear. "The man. I think he was from Dafra?"

The man wore the most whimsical turban that Afia had ever seen, shaped like a crescent moon and hung with all sorts of baubles and trinkets. When he turned his head, Afia's eyes widened.

"Amadi!" she shouted.

The man in the moon-shaped turban stopped mid-sentence, as did everyone else in the room. They all stared at her. The tea kettle in his hand dribbled onto the table. The woman beside him scolded him, and the man set the kettle down.

It was Amadi, the man whom she had seen driven away from Dafra ten years ago. Yet here he was, dressed in colorful clothes and covered in jewelry and pendants. An uncomfortable smile settled on his lips every so often, giving Afia the impression that there was something not quite right about him.

"Your eyes are very familiar to me," he said, drawing closer.

"I'm Afia from Dafra. My sister, Aya, and I were children when—"

"A fellow Dafran!" Amadi interrupted, swarming her with an embrace. "Dear little Afia, look at you! I never could tell you and your twin sister apart." His smile faltered and he searched her face. "But why are you here, child?"

"You have a *twin*?" Ojike whispered in Afia's ear. "You never said."

Amadi must have noticed Afia's unease, because he smiled and said, "Never mind all that. Have some tea with us, won't you?" He took her hand, half pulling, half dancing her over to the head of the table.

The woman beside Amadi shifted the baby in her arms to her hip. "Amadi, dear, will you introduce us to your friend?"

"Oh yes, darling, this is Afia. An old friend from my days in Dafra. Afia, this is my wife, Ndéye."

"En-*day*," the woman enunciated cheerfully, squeezing Afia's hand. "A pleasure to meet you, dear." She turned to the other guests. "We have a newcomer!"

The children encircled Afia, inspecting her travel-worn clothes and asking her a dozen questions at once, while Ndéye piled her plate with food. Everyone else swarmed Afia with cheers and took turns embracing her and introducing themselves—Demba, Masara, Rajendra, Yakuti. Afia couldn't keep up with the rest.

She told them how she had left home and escaped the Queen's palace. The children cheered excitedly upon hearing this, but Afia noticed that some of the adults exchanged nervous glances.

"I told you not to mention that," Ojike whispered peevishly.

But Afia ignored him, quite relieved that the Sonu's interest in her had shifted away from the mention of her sister.

"Who said that?" said Demba, the kora player, looking at her nervously.

"I didn't hear anything," Afia lied.

"Don't mind him, he hears voices." Masara, the writer, grinned.

"And it's nothing to be ashamed about," Ndéye said.

She poured the tea back and forth from the kettle to a small glass, until a thick foam formed at the top. "I hear voices too from time to time, and they're completely harmless."

Afia didn't know what to say to this, so she took a sip from her glass. It was a bitter green tea with just a touch of mint.

When Ndéye moved away to pour more tea, Afia whispered to Amadi, "What about Ilo?"

"Who?" Amadi said, offering her a plate of fruit.

Afia took one absently. Did he not want to discuss his former wife? "Nothing," she said quickly. "I don't mean to pry."

"Pry about what?" Amadi laughed. He looked down at the plate again, before offering it to Afia. "Fruit?"

Before Afia could say anything, everyone drained their teacups, stood up, and traded seats. Ndéye flitted between each guest, doling out a fresh round of tea. The children trailed after her, making a mess wherever they went.

Amadi sat down again and began tinkering with a length of thread, mumbling to himself.

"You have an awful lot of tea things," Afia remarked to Amadi, nodding at the stacks of cups and kettles.

"Wouldn't want anyone to go without!" He held out the plate of fruit again. "How rude of me not to offer you one."

"You did though." Afia frowned. "Twice, actually."

Amadi brightened and returned to the thread in his turban, tangling it and untangling it.

"Ask him how he got here," Ojike whispered.

Afia leaned closer to Amadi, and asked, "Do you remember why you left?"

"Where?"

"Dafra," she said.

"I'm not very good with time," said Amadi. "How long ago was that?"

"Well, I was six."

Amadi looked at her, his smile sagging. "It has been that long, has it? No wonder I'm losing my head."

He reached for a length of embroidered fabric and began to wrap it around his turban.

"What is that you're doing?" Afia asked.

"Keeping my memories from disappearing," he said, pressing the turban against his head and feeling around until he found a silver trinket. "I study each one while repeating the words out loud. They help me remember things. This one, here, is for my family in Dafra," he whispered. "When I touch this bit of silver, I can still feel them. I can still remember the celebration they threw for me when I left."

"That's . . . not what happened," Afia began.

"Really? I remember being outside the gates as the whole town cheered for me and waved me off," Amadi said brightly.

Afia frowned. Something was clearly wrong.

"Don't mind him." Rajendra leaned over and whispered, "Amadi's not been the same since the Queen threw him out. The tea helps a little, but he misses that shape-shifting potion. We all do." Rajendra sighed and proceeded to pour tea into his empty shoe.

Afia looked around. The other Sonu were behaving strangely too. Yakuti was having a conversation with herself, while Demba played the same note over and over on his kora. Across from him, Masara scribbled the same words again and again on sheets of old paper, as though they were the only words worth writing down.

Ojike spoke again. "There has to be a spell over these poor wretches. They could get up and leave Ijábù at any moment, yet they sit here underground."

Afia watched as Ndéye made another round, offering tea and sweets to each of the Sonu, swatting away the hands of the children. Ndéye would look each person in the eye, holding their hand as she asked them the same questions that she had asked them in her previous round. But the Sonu didn't seem to mind, and would answer her with the same enthusiasm as before.

"This round is my favorite," Amadi told Afia as Ndéye filled his cup.

Afia took a sip from hers and grimaced. "That's so sweet!"

Ndéye laughed. "Don't worry, dear. We are going back to a bitter tea soon. We will have many rounds—sweet, bitter, spiced, herbal, floral." She nodded at different guests as she spoke. "That way, we all get to appreciate each other's tastes, while still enjoying our own."

Afia was struck by Ndéye's words, and by how well

the Sonu seemed to get along with one another. There would be a momentary confusion over words or expressions, or the occasional bickering over whether the best dish in all of Djiombé came from where *they* grew up. But these disagreements quickly dissolved into laughter, and the Sonu were soon embracing one another and chattering merrily again.

"How could the Queen dismiss you, when you are all so charming?" Afia said aloud, before she could stop herself. She had meant it as a compliment, but realized that it had not come out that way.

Ojike clicked his tongue, a warning.

"The Queen didn't kick *me* out," said Masara, the writer. "I decided to leave, and she was kind enough to let me."

"Keep telling yourself that," Demba muttered. "The Queen abandoned all of us. She got what she needed from us and threw us out like garbage. She can rot, for all I care."

"We agreed not to speak of this," Amadi said, pulling his turban down over his ears. But the others ignored him.

"Blasphemy!" Yakuti shouted at Demba. "She is still our Queen. She treated us like royalty. I'm sorry, Ndéye, but the palace was far more comfortable than this rabbit's warren."

"How can you praise her? The Queen beheads people," Afia said, growing angry.

Several of the Sonu laughed at this, and Demba gave her a pitying smile. "That's just a rumor."

Afia could not believe what she was hearing.

A sudden breeze began to stir Masara's writing sheets. Everyone gasped as their teacups tipped over of their own accord, spilling their tea. Fruit and pies began flying through the air.

Suddenly, Ojike appeared among the lanterns.

"Are you quite sure that your dear Queen would never behead anybody?" he taunted them. "Then how do you explain this?" His body disappeared, leaving his grinning mask floating above them.

This sent everyone shrieking and racing around in circles.

"It's that awful ghost again!" said Yakuti. "Who let him in?"

Everyone began to shout over one another. Ojike laughed, once again at Afia's side.

Ojike began to chase Rajendra around the table. Masara raced after them, throwing fruit at Ojike but managing to hit Amadi instead. Demba tried to hide under the table, but it was too low to the ground, so he began to pile the floor cushions over himself and his kora. Ndéye shouted at everyone to calm down. All the while, the children giggled and shrieked themselves breathless.

Suddenly, the sound of footsteps reverberated overhead. The Sonu heard this and fell silent.

Everyone looked upward as Ojike returned to Afia's side. The lanterns trembled and large shadows blocked out the sunlight. Then the end of a shovel pierced the ceiling, sending a shower of earth over the table. One of the boys let out a yelp, but Ndéye quickly put a hand over his mouth.

Afia froze. Had she led the guards to the Sonu's hiding place?

"We need to leave," Ojike whispered.

The room descended into chaos as the Sonu dispersed. At Ndéye's command, the children scurried out of the room, carrying armloads of food, dishes, and teacups. Ndéye strapped the baby onto her back and pulled Afia with her into the hall as more of the ceiling collapsed.

"Come with us," Amadi urged Afia.

"I've put you in danger," Afia protested. "But I promise I'll fix it before I return to Dafra. I'm going to break you free of the Queen's spell."

Ndéye frowned. "What spell?"

"There's no time," Ojike hissed.

Amadi stepped forward suddenly and took Afia's hand. "Don't go back to Dafra. You may have been born into the wrong world, but you don't have to stay there." When he saw the look on Afia's face, he smiled sadly. "Follow the tunnel to the right until you reach the gate. Or was it on the left?"

Masara shoved a scroll of old paper into Afia's hand. "It's on the right. The gatekeepers will ask you to recite this."

Afia looked in bewilderment at the scribbled lines. The sound of plates being smashed came from the tea-room behind them.

Ndéye smiled. "This will not be the last time we meet."

Afia turned away, not wanting them to see her tears. Before she and Ojike rounded the bend, she glanced back, but the Sonu were gone. She wondered if Ndéye was right, or if she would never see them again.

20

THE GATEKEEPERS

"How did they find us?" Afia asked Ojike as they hurried through the tunnels.

"I don't know, but you shouldn't have told the Sonu about the spell." Ojike was no longer joking.

"They won't be executed . . . ?" She was afraid to finish the question.

"Only if the Queen finds out they were helping you."

Panic rose in Afia's chest. She never should have agreed to stop there. After all they had been through, the Sonu had managed to carve out a life for themselves here in Ijábù. They were certainly strange, and far from perfect, but they were the only people who had made Afia feel truly at home ever since she'd left Dafra.

After wandering down the same tunnel for what seemed like ages, Afia stopped. "I think we're lost."

"I thought we were going the way they told you to go," Ojike said.

"We are. Aren't you supposed to know your way around here?"

"I've had no reason to visit the Sonu recently," Ojike said defensively. "Besides, there are dozens of these tunnels. I can't be expected to . . ." He paused and began to sniff the air.

"Now what are you doing?" Afia asked.

"Tell me, does it smell different here?"

"I'm not sure," Afia said.

"What about a few paces farther?"

Afia walked forward, sniffing, until she noticed a change in the pungent earthy odor—the smallest hint of a breeze approaching. "It smells clearer here! And it's getting clearer the farther I go." She began to run. "This is the right way, after all."

"I never doubted it," Ojike said, sounding pleased with himself.

"But you didn't know for certain either," Afia pointed out.

Ojike shrugged. "You have a strong aversion to admitting when you're wrong. A common trait among the living."

They continued arguing as the tunnel began to grow brighter. Afia motioned for Ojike to stop. "This must be it!"

In front of them, two masked figures were hunched over a board game next to a gate. They were yelling at each other about the rules, each asserting that *their* version was correct.

"Oh no. Not these two," Ojike whispered as he faded into the air. "They are the worst."

The masked figures glanced up at Afia. "Hello, fair traveler," said the shorter one, seemingly eager to abandon the game. "I am Kasi, and she is Zinzi. Do you wish to leave? I wouldn't blame you if you did . . ."

"What knowledge would you share with us, youthful traveler?" Zinzi interrupted in an irritated tone. "Wisdom is woefully lacking around here, I can assure you."

The two figures turned on each other and began to argue again. Ojike let out a sigh.

Afia hurriedly unrolled the sheet of old paper that Masara had given her. All the words were crossed out, except for one line, which Afia read aloud: *"Kings are only men, and whatever iron cannot achieve against them, words can."* Afia looked up. "May we go now?"

"You're reading," Zinzi said disapprovingly. "That doesn't count."

"You never said I had to have it memorized," Afia answered.

Zinzi sat upright. "I'm saying it now. And besides, we don't use proverbs anymore. They're too easy. Give us an accurate recitation of *The Martyr King*, and we'll let you through." She shook a finger at Afia. "And *no reading*."

"Yes, and you must recite it while bouncing on one foot," Kasi added eagerly.

The two nodded at each other, before looking intently at Afia.

"I've seen them keep people here all day, coming up with new rules," Ojike whispered. "They haven't changed one bit from their palace days."

"I don't have time for this," Afia said, attempting to push past them.

"Careful, girl," Zinzi said. "Who do you think trained the Queen's courtiers? Who do you think filtered out the rubbish?"

"For *months* we protected the standards of her great court. Now we are the keepers of this gate," Kasi shouted, raising what looked like a spear made out of twigs. "If you don't like our rules, then you can leave."

"We would," Ojike said, reappearing. "If you would only let us."

"You!" Zinzi's eyes were wide with recognition. "Who let *you* in?"

"I let myself in," Ojike sneered.

"Which one of you came up with these preposterous rules, anyway?" Afia asked.

"It wasn't me," Kasi said, glaring at Zinzi. "Didn't I tell you that *The Martyr King* was too obscure a work? I don't even know it."

"That's because everything you read makes you cry, and you ruined the pages before you got to the end," Zinzi said with annoyance.

"Well, you're as unfeeling as a rock," Kasi said. "You could've at least stuck to proverbs. At least she knew one of those . . ."

"It's supposed to be difficult," Zinzi snapped. "If anyone can pass, then what's the point of us?"

"Now *that's* the question," Ojike said.

Zinzi glared at Ojike. "Give us one good reason why we should let you pass."

"I have two," Afia said. "You don't have a good reason why we *shouldn't* pass, and your spears are made out of sticks."

Zinzi and Kasi stood there, searching for a rebuttal that never came. Afia walked past them and pushed against the gate. It opened with a shudder of dust and dry leaves.

"What did I tell you?" Ojike laughed. "Rules are never worth following. But I suppose it makes them feel important."

"I can see why you don't get along with them," Afia said. "But why did you quarrel with Amadi and Ndéye?"

"Those two are all right. But the others. You shouldn't have told them that you are going to break the spell, Afia. Some of them are delusional enough to think that the Queen will take them back if they grovel low enough. They will betray you without remorse. That's why I never waste an opportunity to tell them how pathetic they are."

"You're being too hard on them," Afia said crossly. "It's not their fault that the Queen is good at manipulating people."

Ojike laughed. "The Queen only executes people who stand up to her. None of *them* are in any danger of that. They hate me because I'm a reminder of their cowardice."

"You do realize that your current state undermines your position, don't you? I can't imagine many people would want to end up like you."

"Says the one who wants to go home and bury her dreams."

"My dreams were unrealistic," Afia said. "And what's it to you, anyway?"

They continued on for a while in silence.

"You never told me you had a twin," Ojike said, sounding offended.

Afia covered her face. "Please, not you too. I would rather not."

"You'd rather not have a twin, or you'd rather not talk about it?"

"I am not going to answer your ridiculous questions," Afia snapped. "My answer is no. No, to all of them."

Ojike laughed. "No to all of what? I just wanted to know what your sister is like."

This caught Afia by surprise. She thought for a moment. "Aya is endlessly clever, and poised . . . and yet she's the silliest person I've ever met. She's frustratingly good at everything she does, but she is so hard on herself. I used to think that we got along because we are so alike, but we're more different than I ever realized." She shook her head. "I can't explain it. But that's what most people don't understand. They think if they've met one of us, that they know both of us."

"I may never know what being a twin is like," Ojike said gently, "but I do understand how it feels to miss someone."

Afia was surprised by this. "Your brother? Where is he now?"

"It doesn't matter." Ojike shrugged. "We haven't spoken in years."

"I'm sorry." Afia dropped her gaze. She couldn't even remember the last words she had said to Aya before she left. It had all happened so quickly. Had she really lost her sister forever by leaving? She couldn't bear the thought of never hearing her sister's laughter again, or the sound of her voice. Of never speaking to her again.

"No use dwelling on it," said Ojike. "Actually, there's no use dwelling on anything."

"Teach me something, then," Afia said. "How do you know where you're going when all these paths look the same?"

Ojike laughed. "All you have to do is let your feet carry you."

"How easy," Afia said. "Then what do I need you for?"

"*Nothing* is easy. But you need to trust that the knowledge is already within you. This is the same soil that your ancestors walked, you know. You just need to shed all the nonsense that you've piled on top of it."

Afia closed her eyes and took several steps forward, walking directly into a mahogany tree. She looked at Ojike accusingly.

"I didn't say to close your eyes," he jeered. "That says a lot about you, if that's your definition of trust. Follow my voice."

"Are you always this encouraging?"

"Think of it like listening past the surface. But don't just listen with your ears. It's . . . hard to explain."

Afia strained to listen. She heard the sounds of birds

settling down for the evening, the distant sighing of the treetops, the crunching of leaves and branches as animals moved through them. But she couldn't seem to grasp what Ojike was talking about.

"Let's try something else," said Ojike. He was full of energy again, leaping into the air ahead of her. "Come catch me!"

"I can't. You're just air."

"I'm a lot more than that," Ojike said with mock solemnity. "My mask is real, you know."

Afia raced after him, laughing. The faster she ran, the more alive she felt. Darkness was falling, and the forest was coming to life with the sounds of night creatures. But Afia didn't mind now. For the first time in a long while, she felt free.

21

THE CAVE

As Afia ran, a mysterious face appeared between the blur of trees, barely visible in the dusk. It seemed to be watching her, and vanished as soon as she stepped toward it. Afia began to wonder if she had imagined it, but the face appeared again, farther away this time. She couldn't explain why, but it seemed to want to show her something. She rushed after it, not realizing that she was running faster than Ojike.

The face vanished again in front of a cave, where several figures stood holding torches. Afia darted behind a tree to watch. A group of guards was dragging two bird-masked Sonu out of the cave. She recognized the man with the hornbill mask, the one who had offered her his mantle. He was pleading with the guards as they bound his hands and led him away.

Afia's heart pounded. Did the guards know that the hornbill-masked man had helped her? Had his Sonu companions betrayed him, as Ojike had predicted? She had to find Amadi and Ndéye. She had to warn them.

The face appeared again and moved toward the mouth of the cave. Then with one more look back at her, it vanished inside.

Before Afia could follow, Ojike appeared beside her. "You shouldn't run off like that," he scolded. "You could've been captured."

"There was a face in the trees," Afia said. "I think it wanted to show me that the Sonu are in danger."

"So, you've met the unhelpful dead," groaned Ojike. "Don't bother with them. They don't actually *do* anything. They just lead people around in circles, and leave me with all the work."

Afia started toward the cave. "Whatever that spirit is, I think it wants me to go in there to help them."

"You'll never find the Sonu in there, and we don't have time for that, anyway."

"Why should I listen to you?" Afia said angrily. "You said that the guards wouldn't find us in the tunnels, and now they're rounding up the Sonu. If you're not going, then I'll find them myself."

She entered the cave, ignoring Ojike's shouts.

A bright flash caught Afia's eye from the wall, then another, then a dozen more. There were all sorts of treasures and trinkets lodged in the walls and ceiling of the cave. Many were toys made from silver and gold. She wondered who they had belonged to and what they were doing here, embedded in the walls of a cave.

As she moved deeper, the ground fell away beneath her, sending Afia tumbling into the dark. She cried out, and her voice echoed back to her a dozen times.

Afia continued to fall for what felt like a very long while. The gleam of treasures blinked past her like falling stars all the way down. The longer she fell, the slower she seemed to go until she wasn't sure if she was falling at all. Just as she began to wonder about this, Afia landed on a pile of jumbled carpets and tapestries at the bottom of the cave.

Afia got to her feet. Animal bones and fossils lined the walls here instead of trinkets, and stalactites gleamed far above. A small stream of bioluminescent water threw reflections all around the empty cave. Afia began to doubt that any of the Sonu were here. She inspected every corner of the cave but was met with solid stone walls all around.

As she searched the walls, she found a drawing of a gazelle. There was a lion next to it, and a giraffe, and what looked like a zebra. Afia stepped back, and she realized that it was a mural, depicting all kinds of plants and animals—a garden. And in the center of it stood two little girls holding hands. A shiver ran through her.

Everything the Queen had built—her palace, her

garden, her court filled with subjects who wore masks carved after her sister's likeness—it was not merely the whim of an eccentric monarch. It was a tribute to someone that the Queen loved and missed desperately. As Afia gazed at the figures on the wall, she felt a sudden longing to be with Aya again. She couldn't imagine being without her for as long as the Queen had been apart from her sister.

Afia was surprised to realize that she was angry at Aya. For not going with her, for siding with their parents instead of her. For forcing Afia to choose between what she loved and who she loved. Perhaps it was rage, not love, that drove the Queen. Had she also turned her palace into a prison for her sister? Blaming Uzuri for leaving her, and punishing anyone else who came close enough to hurt her? There was something terrifying about how far the Queen had gone, but something sad too. But Afia was not like the Queen—her anger was her own. She could not punish anyone else for a loss that was hers to mourn.

"Afia!" It was Ojike's voice.

She looked around, but he was not there. She followed the sound of his voice to a pale stream of light, where the cavern narrowed to a vertical shaft to the forest above.

"I think the Queen was here once," Afia called back.

"I tried to warn you," Ojike said. "That place is creepy. This is the only way out, so you're going to have to climb up. Do you understand?"

Afia's eyes followed the steep rock wall. It was a long way up. "I don't think I can."

"You have to get out of your head," Ojike's voice urged her. "Look at everything you've done since you left the palace. You'd never done any of it before. And you can do this too."

Afia hesitated, but she had no choice. She began the long, arduous climb. For a moment, Afia slipped, losing her grip on one of the rocks. But she quickly steadied herself and grabbed hold again. Slowly, carefully, she made her way up as Ojike cheered her on.

The passageway narrowed, and the rock walls surrounding her tore at her clothes and skin. Her arms and shoulders burned, and Afia was afraid that her body would give out on her. The hole leading out was too small for her to fit through, so she began to claw at the dirt trapped between the roots of a tree. A torrent of dirt poured over her. She choked and coughed and struggled to breathe, but she continued on, clawing at the earth above her. Her eyes stung and her fingernails throbbed with pain.

"Keep going, Afia, you're almost there," Ojike's voice said. "I promise I'll let you touch my mask if you do this."

Afia broke into a laugh and forgot her exhaustion for a moment. With a final burst, she dug her way through the forest floor and collapsed onto the ground, gasping. Tears streamed from her eyes. She had never been so happy to see the canopy of trees above.

Ojike swarmed her with praise. "You look a mess, but you did it!"

"I have dirt everywhere, in my ears, my nose, my

mouth." Afia laughed. She spat and coughed and shook the dirt out of her hair.

As she got up, she caught sight of one of the mysterious faces watching her with a smile. Then it disappeared. She had the feeling that it had actually been leading her to the painting in the cave, not to the Sonu. But why?

"Let's get you cleaned up," Ojike said, leading her to a river a short distance away.

When she had finished her washing, Afia returned to Ojike's side, clean but shaken. "I saw a drawing on the walls. Of two girls in a garden surrounded by animals. What was the Queen doing down there?"

"Rumor has it that the Queen followed her sister into the forest and got lost," Ojike said. "And she took refuge in that cave." Ojike paused. "Perhaps this is where she devised the plans for her kingdom."

Afia shivered at the thought of being trapped down there. "I'm sorry I ran off."

"If you can blame yourself for your mistakes, then you can at least give yourself credit for your triumphs. You're willing to accept help when it's offered to you."

There was something in the way he said this that made Afia glance up in surprise.

He twirled his mask in front of her. "I promised, didn't I?"

Afia smiled and reached her hand out. The mask was indeed real. She could even feel where the paint had flaked off, leaving bare wood behind.

"You could've left me back there," she said quietly. She reached for his hand and squeezed, even though she could not feel it.

Ojike teased her, "And who would get you home if I did that?"

Afia looked away. "Maybe I shouldn't go home. I'm a terrible sister."

Ojike shrugged. "Turns out I'm not a great brother either. No matter how I tried, I could never get through to him."

"That's how my last conversation with my sister felt. Is it always like this with siblings?"

They shared a glance. Suddenly, Ojike's body

stiffened. Afia had never seen him so agitated. She turned around to see what he was looking at.

A white gazelle stood watching from the shadows on the other side of the clearing. Bakame transformed and strode toward them.

"I'm sorry, Afia," Ojike whispered. Then he vanished.

"He can't see you!" Afia cried out, not understanding why Ojike would abandon her.

Bakame reached her and seized her by the arm. "Who are you talking to?" he said.

"Nobody," Afia said. "No one at all."

22

THE SHRINE

Bakame had caught her at last. Afia struggled and kicked and scratched, but his grip was strong. Without another word, he bound her wrists and led her away through the trees.

Afia looked around desperately, but Ojike did not reappear. She had misjudged him. That angered her.

"What are you up to? Why aren't the guards with you?" she demanded.

Bakame gave her a withering look and continued on quickly. His sense of urgency should have frightened her, but Afia found herself intrigued.

They reached a small house in a clearing. The neat row of flower beds outside the door looked startlingly out of place against the wild trees.

Inside, Bakame unfastened her binds and told her to clean herself up. He left the room before she could say anything. She caught her reflection in a large standing mirror. What had once been a beautiful ball gown was now torn and discolored. Cuts and bruises laced her body, and a particularly nasty cut stung her cheek. She pressed her fingers against it. Behind a folding screen there was a bath, a stunning court gown, new sandals, and a comb. Afia put on the sandals, ignoring the rest.

She looked around. The house was understated, nothing like the extravagance of the palace. A small table and a lone chair stood before the hearth, and a row of books lined one wall.

Afia's eyes fell on a small alcove beside the window. There, delicately arranged, stood dozens of animal sculptures carved from wood and amber. One figure sat in the middle of the display on a length of cloth, surrounded by a string of glass beads, small animal bones, and candles. It was a funerary shrine.

The figure at the center was carved with rough strokes, which made it feel almost alive. Its shape was unmistakable. It was a grinning wildcat.

Afia stood there in a daze. They were *brothers*. How could Ojike keep this from her? How could Bakame?

The door opened, and Bakame entered the room. Afia kept her face very still.

Bakame looked at her tattered dress, then at the new sandals on her feet. "Still the rebel, I see. I must admit, you are stronger than I took you for." He poured wine into a pair of goblets and offered her one.

"I don't need your approval," she said. It took all her strength to keep her mounting anger in check.

Bakame shook his head. "I was paying you a compliment. I hope you've realized by now that I was right. This is no life for you. You've inflicted a great wound on the Queen, but if you beg for her forgiveness, I will see to it that you can still enter her court."

"I would rather die," Afia said coldly.

A look of concern passed over Bakame's face. "I'm

the only one who can protect you. But you must come back with me at once—"

Afia cut him off. "Like you protected Ojike? Why should I trust a man who serves the murderer of his own brother?"

Bakame looked stricken. "How did you know about that?"

Afia hesitated. She had wanted to hurt him, but when she saw the grief in his eyes, she began to regret her words. "Your brother helped me escape," she said quietly. "Please, let me go home."

Bakame spoke without looking at her. "I did not come to bargain with you, Afia. I did what I could for Ojike and am offering the same to you now. When the Queen's guards find you, they will not offer you such mercy."

"Where is the choice in that?" Afia said, growing angrier. "And why are you hiding from your brother? Why won't you speak to him?" She reached for his talismans.

Bakame recoiled. "He is dead! What more is there to say?" He hurled his goblet across the room. "Get out."

Afia ran to the door and out of the house, not stopping even when she reached the forest. She was furious at herself. How had she missed every hint, every clue that was so obvious to her now?

But one thing was as certain as her anger. She had to find Ojike.

23

THE RIFT

Ojike found Afia first. He sounded relieved. "I was beginning to think that you were on your way to the Queen's dungeon by now."

Afia turned on him. "You lied to me."

"What are you talking about?" Ojike laughed, but his body began to disappear.

"Don't you dare," Afia said. "Why didn't you tell me that Bakame was your brother?"

"You didn't ask."

Afia laughed bitterly. "You two are quite the pair, aren't you? Telling half-truths whenever it suits you and then blaming me for not asking the right questions. Did you forget that he's the reason why I'm here?"

Ojike made a small sound, but Afia cut him off.

"You knew that if you told me who your brother was, that I would never help you break the spell. Well, you were right." She crossed her arms. "This is over. Take me home right now."

"That was not our bargain," Ojike began.

"I don't care."

"You don't understand." Ojike hung his head. "Bakame never would have met the Queen if it wasn't for me. I was the one who convinced him to leave the caravan and find a patron for his carvings. I told him about a powerful queen of Ijábù, who was seeking the greatest talents from across Djiombé. A year later, I found him in her court, but I hardly recognized him. Bakame is not even his real name—he had 'reinvented' himself. We had a quarrel, and I'm not proud of the words I said . . . He fell deeper into the Queen's service after that. So you see, I'm the one you should blame for what he's become. And I owe it to him and everyone he's lured into Ijábù to set him free."

"Bakame is responsible for them, not you," Afia said. "I'm sorry, but you need to find someone else to help you."

"There *is* no one else," Ojike shouted. "Everyone in this horrible place has either surrendered to the Queen or is too much of a coward to do anything about it. And here you are, the only one who's ever escaped without being spellbound, and you're going to give up? Are you really going to run back home and hide from the world again? Bakame didn't make you do anything you didn't want to do, did he?"

"Are you defending him?" Afia asked fiercely.

"I'm merely pointing out that you are both to blame. Your sister didn't follow him, did she?"

Afia's eyes narrowed. That was too far. "Take me home. Now."

Ojike wrung his hands. "You are so stubborn! Going back to your sister won't solve anything. You're not the same anymore, and neither is she. The moment you left, everything changed. I think you know that."

Afia was too angry to speak. She turned away and

left him there, ignoring his shouts. She should never have trusted him. Nor Bakame, nor the Queen.

She didn't know how long she walked, but by the time Afia stopped, she was certainly lost. The trees loomed hundreds of feet overhead, taller than any she had encountered before. The forest was becoming dark and the sounds of the night swelled all around her. But perhaps being alone wasn't so bad. At least here, no one could hurt her.

The sky opened with a crack of rain. But Afia continued on, even as the ground grew slick with mud. She was done being dependent, she was done asking for help, for permission, or for guidance. She didn't need anyone. She would find her own way.

As the darkness grew, Afia could no longer see the ground through the downpour, nor the sprawling roots of the mahogany tree that rose in a sharp angle. She stumbled and put out her hands to break her fall. The string of the bracelet that her sister had given her caught on the sharp end of a branch and snapped, sending amber beads flying.

Afia cried out and began fumbling through the mud. But she only managed to recover a single bead. The rain fell harder, forcing her to take refuge beneath a tree root, holding the little bead tightly. She felt small and alone, and she wept out of guilt for losing the only thing she had left of her sister.

She wished she hadn't driven Ojike away. What was worse, he had been right. Ijábù *had* changed her, and her departure from Dafra had undoubtedly changed Aya too. The childhood that they'd shared was gone, and even if she went back home now, neither of them could ever return to how things were before.

She mourned everything that could have been, had she not grown up in fear of disappointing her family. If she had dared to tell Aya about the life she wanted sooner, her sister might have been angry at first, but maybe she would have understood. And though her mother had never asked her what she wanted for her future, Afia had never shown her true self to her family either. Perhaps her mother had always been hard on her because she had sensed that. No wonder the distance between her and her family had become insurmountable.

She thought about everyone she had met in Ijábù. She thought of Amadi, Ndéye, and the Sonu having to start over again. Of her dancing partner's nameless grave under the ìrókò trees. And of Ojike's continued love for Bakame and his desire to set him free.

Afia began to cry again. Then she remembered her father's words. *There's nothing wrong with having a good cry, unless that's all you intend to do.* Her father had always been a quiet champion of Afia's curiosity, always answering her questions and softening her mother's criticism however he could. Afia saw his strength more clearly now.

The first rays of dawn strained through the steady rain. Afia wiped her eyes. She didn't know what she would do now, but she wouldn't sit here and wallow anymore.

She tied the amber bead around her neck and got to her feet.

24

THE MUSHROOM FOREST

Afia did not know how much time had passed. She was past the point of exhaustion and she didn't know where she was going, but she pushed on through the dense trees.

She remembered Ojike's advice about how to navigate the forest. *All you have to do is let your feet carry you.* She went haltingly along at first, but then she began to notice details in her path. A slight curve of the earth here, a worn patch of vegetation there. She found what appeared to be half an elephant's footprint, then another. The faster she went, the more animal footprints she saw along the same trail—mammals, birds, and reptiles, all heading in the same direction.

As she followed this path, Afia felt a shift in the energy around her. The sounds and vibrations of the forest all blended together like a language that she didn't understand but that she felt connected to. All at once, a host of ancient faces shimmered into view. They reminded her of the one that she had seen outside the cave. The faces moved silently through the trees, watching her, surrounding her. Were they spirits of the Queen's dead, or of the trees themselves?

They guided her on until she reached a thicket of strange trees in a cloud of blue haze. As she drew closer, Afia noticed that they were not trees at all but enormous mushrooms. There were hundreds rising above her in all directions.

Afia couldn't believe she had found the mushroom forest. Had the footprints led her here? Or had the ghostly faces? She turned around to ask them, but they were no longer there.

The blue mist grew thicker and more pungent, and the treelike mushrooms gave way to smaller ones that carpeted the ground and glowed in bioluminescent hues. Afia knelt down to inspect them.

"Who are you?" said a deep voice from above her.

There, atop a mushroom that was almost as tall as her, sat a strange figure smoking a pipe. Afia knew this must be Sékou, the shaman.

"This is a sacred place," Sékou said. "If you dare enter here, you must answer this question. So tell me, who are you?"

"I'm Afia of Dafra."

"That means nothing to me if it means nothing to you."

Afia laughed. "Of course it does. That's my name."

"I don't care about your name. I asked who you are."

Afia frowned. "I'm Aya's sister . . . her twin sister. Daughter of Thema and Ime. Granddaughter of Musu."

"Is that all?" the shaman said. "How disappointing." He turned away.

"My answers are true. I don't understand what you want from me."

"Then you know nothing about yourself," Sékou said simply, with a great, smoky exhalation.

She scoured her mind for wisdom from Master Fọlámí's lessons, but the words she had absorbed for so many years now seemed to crumble before her.

"I am not interested in the words of dead men," the shaman said, as though he were reading her thoughts.

"Ojike was right," Afia muttered. "You *are* condescending."

"That still doesn't answer the question."

"I'm alone in an enchanted forest, I'm sixteen years old, and I can't do anything by myself. There, is that it?"

"If you cannot do anything yourself, then you really are nothing."

"Then I am nothing," Afia agreed. "Are you satisfied yet?"

Sékou shrugged. "So far, all you've given me are irrelevant facts, evasions, and self-pitying nonsense. All are poor substitutes for truth." He seemed to be losing interest again and began to puff long tendrils of smoke.

"I'm here to break the Queen's spell," Afia said, with growing desperation. "Please, I'm the only one who can do this."

Sékou seemed unimpressed. "How would you know? You can't even tell me who you are."

Afia slumped to the mushroom-covered ground and covered her face with her hands. Why did Ojike think she could save anyone? She wished that she had never left home or dreamed of the world beyond Dafra.

"Self-pitying," the shaman said.

"Get out of my head!" Afia snapped.

But of course he was right. "I thought I knew the answer to your question," she said at last. "But it turns out, I don't. I know who my family wanted me to be. I know who I thought I was. But I'm still figuring the rest out."

Sékou puffed on his pipe for some time, making a soft humming sound, and Afia wondered if he had fallen asleep while smoking.

"Forgetting can be necessary," Sékou said abruptly. "Forgetting can be useful. Only truth remains in an immutable form. So tell me, Afia of Dafra. What remains of you, after you rid yourself of everything that came before?"

An overwhelming sadness suddenly descended over Afia, and her hand flew to the amber bead at her neck. "Before I knew anything about myself, I knew I had a sister. We were born together. Do I have to forget her too?"

"No, that's good. What else?"

The words tumbled out of her. "Birds and trees and water, the night sky, the air in my lungs, and the thrill of discovering new and wonderful things."

Sékou swished his pipe in the air, speaking between streams of smoke. "If you want to know the end, you must look to the beginning."

The ground seemed to pulse beneath her, and the sea of mushrooms vibrated with a bright blue light. Afia closed her eyes. Something that had lain dormant within her for years stirred beneath the surface. She surrendered to it.

The sound of childish laughter filled her ears. She saw herself and Aya as little girls, darting among the Dafran cliffs, pretending that they were long-lost royalty born of the trees and earth. She saw her own crude drawings of wild wonderlands that she had dreamed up. Afia had been an intrepid explorer as a child, determined to discover every insect that crawled, every leaf, rock, and flower.

The memories came faster now. Their mother had taken them to visit the mines. Afia had wandered off, following the crystal veins that glittered against the walls. She remembered when she'd realized that her sister was not beside her for the first time. The darkness that surrounded her. And when her mother had finally found her, Afia had begged her to sew her hands to her sister's so that she would never be parted from her again.

The vision showed her something else—Aya had wept, promising to never lose Afia again, but she had borne their mother's blame ever since. Aya had given up her own childhood to become Afia's protector. Did Aya resent her? Had she too longed for her own sense of self, apart from her sister?

Afia opened her eyes. The overwhelming sadness welled within her, for the loss of her childhood, her family, and what would never be again between her and her sister. But there was relief too, and it washed over her. She answered Sékou's question at last. "I am Afia of Dafra. I used to let my curiosity lead me, before it was replaced by fear. Perhaps I will again."

Sékou nodded. He pointed to a mushroom in front of her with his pipe. "You may take a bite," he said.

Afia pulled the mushroom up by its root. Its bright white stalk pulsed as though it had a tiny bioluminescent heart. She closed her eyes and bit into the cap.

Nothing happened at first. Then she noticed with some alarm that her feet were no longer touching the ground. The blue smoke had been making her feel increasingly lightheaded, but now she couldn't tell if she was awake or dreaming.

Afia began to float into the air. She cried out, but Sékou ignored her. She went on soaring, higher and higher, until she burst through the forest ceiling. To her surprise, above that ceiling was another, and then another. Canopy upon canopy of trees took her breath away, each a universe unto itself.

Hundreds of brightly colored birds flocked around her. The branches bent under the weight of fruit and flowers, swarmed by troops of monkeys, chameleons, and other animals. Hawks and eagles swooped in and out. She flew through a cloud of brilliantly painted butterflies that brushed her face with their wings.

At last, Afia crested the treetops. A tranquil sea of green stretched below her, without a wave or a ripple. Far away, a silver ribbon gleamed in the light—a river.

Perhaps the same one that she had braved after her escape from the palace. The serenity overwhelmed her. She could just make out the sprawling gray shape of the Queen's palace. How ugly it looked from here, against the sea of living, breathing green. But something else lay beyond it—faint blue mountains, distant lands and seashores, and faraway cities.

There was a world beyond Ijábù, with wonders yet to be seen. What the Queen had offered her hadn't been her dream at all. There was no sign of Dafra beyond the endless swath of forest. She marveled at how far she had traveled and wondered why she had ever doubted herself.

Suddenly, her body sank below the canopy again. She plummeted downward faster and faster. Birds and branches blurred past. She squeezed her eyes shut, waiting for the impact. Pungent smoke filled her nose again, and to her surprise, her body stopped inches above the mushrooms and dropped softly to the ground.

Afia noticed that she was holding the mushroom that she had bitten into. Somehow, it was still whole. She looked up at Sékou. "I thought . . . What just happened?"

"That's the wrong question," he said, puffing on his pipe. "All that matters is what you will do now." With a satisfied air, Sékou turned to leave.

Just then, Ojike burst into the clearing. It was clear to Afia that he had been watching the entire time.

"How do we break the spell?" he asked Sékou eagerly. "How do we stop the Queen's magic?"

Sékou drew back. "Nettlesome sprite, must I banish you to the stars to be rid of you?"

"I'm sorry, Afia," Ojike said, sounding embarrassed. "But I was very patient, and you weren't going to ask him—"

"There is no spell!" Sékou bellowed. "It is true that the Queen knows magic—I taught it to her many years ago." He lowered his head a little. "She was still a child and did not appear to have ill intent. But her greatest skill is manipulation, not sorcery. Her courtiers could stop drinking that potion and be free of her whenever they like."

"What of my brother's talismans?" Ojike insisted. "The Queen forces him to wear them. Can we at least free him?"

Sékou gave Ojike a pitying look. "Your brother begged the Queen for those talismans. Why do you suppose he wears so many, when everyone else only wears one?"

Ojike was struck silent. Indeed, for the first time since Afia had known him, he seemed at a loss for words, and drifted forlornly away.

"Wait, Ojike!" Afia called after him. She murmured a thank-you to the shaman, but he was making a deep humming sound again and did not appear to hear her.

She reached Ojike just in time to see him climb into a tree and fade into the branches. "Ojike, I'm sorry." When he didn't answer, she continued, "I understand what it feels like to be wrong about someone, but you can't stay up there forever."

His voice came quietly. "I shouldn't have wasted your time. I should have just guided you home like you asked."

"I'm glad you didn't. I'm sorry it didn't turn out like you hoped, but at least you know the truth now."

Ojike suddenly reappeared and leaped out of the tree. "You could talk to Bakame for me," he said, taking her hand. "He likes you, you know. You could convince him to throw his talismans away."

Afia gave him an incredulous look. "He would never listen to *me*."

“Maybe you can get close enough to him and rip the talismans off,” Ojike begged. “Please, Afia.”

No sooner had he said those words than there came the sound of ironclad footsteps, closing in from every direction.

25

THE CAPTURE

The Queen's guards descended on her so quickly that Afia did not even have time to move. In an instant, she was surrounded by a wall of iron armor and bloodred capes.

"Spineless sandal-lickers!" Ojike sprang at them, hissing.

But the guards were wearing talismans and could not hear or see him. Afia reached for the neck of the nearest guard and tried to rip his talisman from him. But he grabbed her hands and held them behind her back.

“You are to be taken to the dungeon to await trial,” a female guard said.

“For what?” Afia laughed.

The guard behind her began binding Afia’s wrists without answering her.

Afia waited for Bakame to arrive and mock her. But he was nowhere to be seen.

“I’m right here,” Ojike’s voice said, close to her ear. “It’s got to make you feel special, seeing that the Queen sent her entire force after you.”

Afia could tell that he was doing his best to cheer her up. But he could not hide the fear in his voice.

“I was put on trial too,” he whispered. “That means the Queen likes you enough to let you reconsider instead of executing you immediately.”

“That’s a comforting thought,” Afia said. “Isn’t there anything you can do?”

“I can follow you to the palace, but I can’t go in because of the talismans.”

Afia remembered the string of talismans above the door she had used to escape the dungeon. How she wished she had thought to tear them down.

One of the guards stopped the column. Afia froze. There, looking back at her, were Amadi, Ndéye, and the rest of their Sonu family, bound together wrist to wrist.

The forest blurred past as they walked. Afia had failed everyone, including herself. And if it really was up to each courtier, every guard, and every one of the Sonu to free themselves from the Queen's influence, then perhaps the Queen had already won.

A pair of ancient eyes caught her gaze through the trees. Then another, then a dozen more. The faces that had guided her to the mushroom forest accompanied her now to the Queen's palace. Afia had a strange feeling that they wanted her to go there, just like they had wanted her to find Sékou. She didn't understand why, but the serenity in their faces gave her a small amount of consolation.

26

THE DUNGEON

Afia was taken to the palace dungeon, down the same hallway with many doors that she had wandered through before. The portrait of the Queen's sister was still there, watching over the dungeon with a smile that now seemed to mock Afia.

She turned in time to see Ndéye, Amadi, and the other Sonu being led to a cell at the far end of the hall.

"What are they here for?" Afia asked the guard beside her.

"Treason, same as you," the guard said roughly. He shoved Afia into a cell and left without another word.

Afia sank to the floor. It was cold and dark, and she could hear the sound of faint weeping through the walls. Would she leave the palace through the small door for a second and final time? Would the Sonu follow her?

Afia did not know what she feared more—facing the Queen or the death that awaited her. She was filled with regret, anger, terror . . . but mostly sorrow for her family, who would never know that she had tried to go back to them. That even though she had left, she still loved them.

A shadow fell over her. Afia looked up.

There, on the other side of the bars, stood Bakame. She caught him staring at the cuts on her arms and at her ruined gown.

"Are you here to gloat?" she asked.

"You're just as stubborn as my brother was." Then Bakame said something that took her by surprise. "I'm sorry. I never should have brought you here."

Afia laughed bitterly. "Save your regrets for my execution."

Bakame dropped to his knees. "Afia, listen to me." There was an edge of desperation in his voice. "Ojike let his pride determine his fate. The Queen will humiliate you at the trial tomorrow. She will make an example out of you. Joining her court is the only way out. Deceive her, if you must. But if you serve her well, you will make a good life for yourself here. I promise."

Afia cut him off. "Listen to yourself! You let her kill your brother, and yet you continue to grovel before her. Did you care for him at all?"

When Bakame spoke, his voice was barely a whisper. "I buried Ojike myself. I couldn't let the King be the one to do it. The Queen refused to give me his head, so I carved a mask for him. He always reminded me of a wildcat . . ." He looked away, but Afia could see that his eyes were bright with tears.

Even though she was angry at Bakame, Afia regretted her words. The young man in front of her was broken with grief and sincerity and was nothing at all like the Queen's manipulative servant.

"How did it happen?" she asked.

"Our parents are proud people; they expected greatness from both of us. Ojike was just a boy, selfish, erratic, and devilishly curious about the world. He decided early on that rules did not apply to him. I wanted that freedom too, but I was left to support our parents.

"Ojike always loved my sculptures, and he truly believed I would find success. But when I finally did find success, it was here at the palace. The gold

I sent home was more than either of my parents had ever seen.

"When Ojike found me here, he mocked me for wanting an easy life, as he called it. *He* was the one who had it easy. Ojike could just be himself and people would help him, give him things. I think he expected that would work on the Queen as well, that he could charm her. But he didn't realize who he was dealing with.

"Can you believe he laughed when the Queen ordered his execution? He was a rebel to the end. I begged him to take the potion, but he waved me off. He told me I had sold out. That I had given up the only thing that he liked about me. I was so angry, I walked away. I should have swallowed my pride. I should have found a way to save him."

Bakame paused, and to Afia's surprise, he reached for her hand through the bars and held it tightly. "Don't do what my brother did," he pleaded. "He was a lucky fool until his luck ran out. You've seen how serious the Queen is, so you can't claim ignorance like he did. Please, Afia. I can't lose someone like this again."

Afia was suddenly embarrassed for suggesting that Bakame alone could have prevented Ojike's execution, before the Queen and her guards and the entire court.

"Your brother wants to see you again," she said gently. "He helped me escape the palace because he thought that you were under a spell, that the Queen was forcing you to wear those talismans."

Bakame's hand trembled.

"Ojike knows there is no spell now. He also knows that the talismans protecting the palace are the only thing keeping him out."

Bakame did not look at her. "The Queen ordered me to carve them."

Afia shook her head. "After all those years you spent mastering your skills, she's reduced you to making charms for her. She doesn't care about you at all."

"Of course she doesn't," Bakame said vehemently. "But she *values* me. She relies on me, more than she relies on the King, even."

"That carving at your house, the one you made for Ojike. She's forced you to give up carving anything you care about. How is that valuing you?"

"Think what you will of me, Afia, but I can't go back to being a failed carver. Not after losing my brother. It all had to be for something." He got to his feet. "If you intend to live, then you know what you must do tomorrow."

Afia gripped his arm through the bars. "Your sculptures mean something to your brother. They mean something to me too. Your failure was giving them up."

Bakame hesitated. Then he pulled away from her and disappeared down the hall, taking the last of Afia's hope with him.

27

THE TRIAL

Bakame arrived the next morning with two guards. He looked like he hadn't slept. When he met Afia's eyes, he seemed to want to say something, but he hung back as the guards led Afia out of her cell and out of the dungeon.

A wall of red-caped guards parted to allow them into the throne room. The walls were now hung with bloodred tapestries, and the harsh white light from the windows sliced through the room in diagonal shafts. Afia couldn't believe that only a short while ago she had stood in the same room, overwhelmed with wonder.

Ndéye, Amadi, and the rest of the Sonu stood among the crowd of onlookers, surrounded by guards. Amadi's turban had become so heavy with fabric that he could not raise his head to look at Afia as she passed. Ndéye gave her a weak smile and hushed the baby in her arms.

Bakame kept his head down as he took his place to the Queen's right. On the left, a jury of courtiers dressed in red sneered as Afia reached the throne.

King Ekwe rose and read aloud from a scroll. "Here stands the accused, Afia of Dafra. She is guilty of high treason against Queen Ukiwa of Ijábù, a crime punishable by death." The King cleared his throat. "Our gracious Queen offers the accused a last chance at her life." He frowned, as if he did not believe that Afia deserved this. "Accept the Queen's hand as her loyal courtier, or lose your head."

The executioner stood beside the Queen, his axe

gleaming in his hands. A servant brought forward a small bottle of red liquid and placed it on a podium before the throne. All heads turned toward Afia.

Afia closed her eyes, trying to calm herself. She tried to imagine what Ojike's last thoughts had been, what he had felt, standing where she stood now. Had he been as frightened as she was? She thought about the drawings she had seen in the cave, of a beautiful garden with two sisters hand in hand. The little girl who had made those drawings had been alone and afraid in a strange land. The courtiers, the Sonu, and even Afia feared the Queen, but it was the Queen who was the most afraid of all. Afia thought she had left fear behind by leaving Dafra, but there were fearful people here too. One thing was certain, however. Neither she nor anyone she had ever met had been born into fear. They had learned it.

The room was quiet. Afia opened her eyes. She had already decided—she would not remain among fearful people any longer, starting with herself.

Afia stepped toward the podium, locked eyes with the Queen, and knocked the bottle to the ground. It shattered, staining the floor with red. A collective gasp ripped through the court.

The Queen regarded her coldly, a smile forming on her lips. She lifted a hand, and the room fell silent. "My dear Afia," she said in a wounded voice, "I gave you everything. All I wanted was love in return. But what did you do instead? You abandoned me. You are a selfish girl. You choose death, because you do not value love."

"I choose neither you nor death," Afia said.

The crowd began to murmur.

"You don't love any of us, so how could we love you in return?" Afia continued. "When you grow tired of us, you banish us. When we refuse you, you behead us. That's how afraid you are. Afraid of us leaving you."

A hush fell over the court. Even the King was speechless. The Queen sat very still, never taking her eyes off Afia. She raised her hand to the executioner.

Bakame spoke up. "My Queen, I think you should reconsider—"

The Queen turned to look at him amusedly. "After everyone who has gone before, why would you have me reconsider *her* fate? Come now, Bakame. You are smarter than this. You have given up so much to be here. What is it about this insignificant creature that makes you waver now?" The Queen laughed. "You didn't even speak up on behalf of your own brother."

Bakame looked stunned. He gave a curt bow and walked away from the throne.

"How disappointing," the Queen muttered to her court, loud enough for Bakame to hear. "He's become quite dull, hasn't he?"

The King smirked, and a few of the courtiers tittered as Bakame left the room.

"Now, where were we?" the Queen said airily. "Ah, yes. Do you have any last words, my dear?"

Afia looked calmly at the many faces staring back at her. "The Queen's lies are her true power, but you don't need to drink them anymore. You see how little she values her most trusted servant. It doesn't matter how high you climb in her court. The Queen keeps a magnificent palace and loyal subjects to lure her sister here—the only person she *really* cares for. You mean nothing to her beyond that."

The court broke into a flurry of whispers again. Some looked dazed. Others let out shouts of protest.

"I told you she was a tyrant!" Demba said to Masara, before being suppressed by one of the guards.

Afia glanced back at the Queen. The look of amusement on Ukiwa's face quickly turned to rage. Then the Queen's eyes fixed on something behind Afia.

Afia turned to see the guards arguing with someone at the door. It was Bakame. There was a wild look in his eyes.

"What is it now?" the Queen demanded.

Bakame did not answer. He reached Afia's side, and with a swift motion, he drew his carving knife and cut her binds. Then he reached into the folds of his tunic and withdrew the broken pieces of something wooden. He threw them to the floor and glared at the Queen.

Afia recognized the pieces on the ground. They were

the broken pieces of the talismans that had hung outside the palace.

The Queen's eyes widened with rage. "Off with his head!" she screamed.

The whole room shuddered and echoed with mischievous laughter. An unseen force struck the guards on their heads and pulled the spears out of their hands.

Ojike's grinning mask appeared overhead, followed by the rest of him. He careened around the room like a loose arrow, heckling the guards, who had not thought to wear their talismans within the safety of the palace. He leaped toward the executioner with a maniacal shout. "Hello, old friend!"

The executioner took one look at him and fled.

When he reached the Queen, Ojike removed his mask with an exaggerated bow, exposing his severed neck. The entire court reacted in horror. Some covered their faces, others screamed. The Queen sat frozen to her seat. Bakame, still wearing his talismans, trembled as he watched their reactions.

"I had hoped you'd remember me," Ojike jeered at the Queen. "There are a few others who would like to pay their respects." Everyone followed his gaze to the open door as a host of a hundred ghostly faces sailed into the room.

The crowd descended into chaos. The jury disbanded, and many courtiers took flight.

The Queen leaped to her feet. "Fools! There is nothing for you out there." When they did not stop, she shouted, "Off with their heads!" but the guards ignored her as they hurried toward the door. "Stop! Come back here at once, or—"

"Or what? You'll take *all* their heads?" a voice said. It was Ojike, drifting past the throne. "You'll still be alone, you know . . ." he said, before vanishing.

The Queen sank back into her seat, mumbling, "Don't leave. Don't leave."

As Afia approached the Queen, the King blocked her path. She looked into his eyes. "Why do you still protect her? You've given her everything. But what has that gotten you? She doesn't even see you."

The King staggered back as if Afia had struck him.

The throne room was in shambles, and most of the assembled onlookers and courtiers had deserted it. Afia stood face-to-face with the Queen. "After all the lives you've taken, was it worth it? Are you any less alone?"

The Queen averted her eyes, but Afia could see that she was trembling.

As Afia turned to leave, the Queen called out to her in a thin voice. "You may try to explain to your sister why you left, but it won't matter. It will never be enough to repair what you've done."

Afia turned back. "That is for her to decide. If she's the person that I know, then she will someday understand how hard it was for me to leave. After she sifts through the pain, only one fact will remain—that I love her, and I always will."

The defeated look on Ukiwa's face was the last that Afia saw of her.

Outside the palace, some of the courtiers were pulling off their headdresses, looking around absently.

Some splashed and cavorted in the fountains, drenching their fine clothes. Several of the guards sliced the rose hedges with their spears, helping a group of Sonu and courtiers make their way out of the garden and toward the forest.

Amadi, Ndéye, and the Sonu surrounded Afia and embraced her. "We destroyed the potions," they shouted gleefully.

Ojike was in hysterics. "We watered her roses with them!"

Some of the courtiers went back into the palace and

came out carrying musical instruments, which they handed out to courtiers and Sonu alike. The man with the hornbill mask and the other bird-masked Sonu broke into a celebratory dance, throwing their masks and mantles aside.

Demba, Rajendra, Masara, and Yakuti were having a picnic on a shredded piece of curtain, offering meat pies to anyone who passed. Ndéye and Amadi poured out tea into golden goblets for everyone, laughing and chatting as they went around.

Afia took a goblet and joined the dancers.

Later, when Afia found Bakame in the courtyard, he was sitting alone watching the festivities around him.

Afia put a hand on his shoulder.

Bakame was silent. Then he cast his talismans away, one by one. He looked up at Afia. "Can you take me to him?"

Afia smiled and helped him to his feet.

28

A NEW BEGINNING

The forest was brilliant and green in the morning light, as though Ijábù itself had expelled the gray mists that shrouded it.

When they reached the ìrókò grove, Bakame glanced at her nervously. Afia nodded.

He lowered his eyes. "My dear brother, there are so many things I wish I had done differently . . . Please, I would like to see you."

"I may be persuaded," Ojike said, appearing between the branches, "if you groveled a little lower, Bakame. Or should I say, Ikenna?"

Bakame glanced up with a grin. Then, upon seeing the mask that he had carved, he hid his face and wept.

Ojike seemed quite moved too and put his arms around Bakame. Afia watched the brothers with a hint of sadness. She knew that even if her sister did come around, it would take time. But Afia would be ready, no matter how long that might be.

Bakame looked over at her, noticing how quiet she was. "I want you to have this." He took something from his tunic and pressed it into her hands. "Something to remember us by."

It was the wildcat figure that he had made for his brother's shrine. Afia ran her fingers over it. Bakame had never carved anything more beautiful.

"I hope this means that I'll see more of your carvings soon," she said.

Bakame smiled. "I have much to atone for here, but perhaps someday I can grant you that wish."

Afia moved through the forest alone. She didn't know the way out of Ijábù, but she knew she would find it.

She reached a clearing, at the center of which stood an ancient tree. She wondered how many travelers it had seen, and how many lost ones had walked past without seeing it. She ran her hand over the bark and felt warmth beneath the surface.

She closed her eyes and took a deep breath. Only the sound of insects filled her ears at first. But the steady whir fell back to reveal a tapestry of sounds, of millions of insects, plants, and animals living and breathing in unison, each one pulsing with life. She felt connected to them, to her ancestors, and to everything that had ever lived and breathed.

When Afia let go of the tree, her fingers still buzzed with warmth. She opened her eyes. The ghostly faces that had guided her through Ijábù were there, watching her. She looked behind herself. A circle of trees stood across the clearing, each with a hole cut through the center. Doorways leading to other lands.

"They have always been there, you know." It was a voice she had grown to love and would miss terribly.

Ojike chuckled. "I was going to show you the way out, but it looks like you found it on your own. So it's back to Dafra, then?"

"Not yet," Afia said. "You were right. It's time that I follow my own path." She reached for his hand. "I don't suppose I'll see you again."

"It's for the best, you know, and I must say I'm proud of you," Ojike said. "If you are ever in need of tormenting, you know where to find me."

"I won't ever forget you."

"I owe you a bigger debt," he said quietly. "Go on, then, you've earned this." He gestured to the circle of trees before vanishing.

Afia stood alone for a moment, watching the place where her friend had stood. She squeezed the wildcat figure in her hands. Then she stepped through one of the trees and was again enveloped by mist.

When she emerged on the other side, she felt a great

sense of relief. She looked back, and the hole in the tree was gone. She was at the edge of a forest that looked no different from any other.

Afia reached the top of the hill and took in the vista of rolling savannahs and magnificent cities gleaming on the horizon. She had always wondered what the sun might look like shining over distant lands. She broke into ecstatic laughter. No one was there to share in her triumph, but she didn't mind. She would write to her sister. She would tell her all about her first adventure, and all her future ones.

Afia heard a familiar shout and looked up to see Ndéye, Amadi, and the Sonu rushing over to her. They seemed happier than when she had first met them. Amadi's turban even looked a bit lighter.

"How wonderful to see you here!" Amadi said. "Where are you traveling to?"

Afia grinned. "Anywhere in need of exploration."

"May we join you?" Ndéye said. The children surrounding her nodded and begged.

"I would love nothing more," Afia said.

EPILOGUE

Afia gazed out over the market. Buyers in bold, colorful prints stood out against the Dafran vendors in white. As she moved past stalls, both familiar and new, a hush settled over the people who she passed.

The crystal stall came into view. Afia had dreamed of this moment many times. An old, familiar fear crept into her stomach. But it was not her mother standing at the stall. It was Aya, graceful as ever, chatting happily to a young family who had stopped to admire a display of crystal jewelry—clearly Aya's own designs.

But just beyond a row of fine bracelets, something else caught Afia's eye. It was the carved gazelle she had left behind, the one that Bakame had given her. Her sister had kept it with her all this time. Afia squeezed the wildcat figure in her hand to steady herself.

At that moment, Aya glanced up. Their eyes met.

And Afia found that she was no longer afraid.

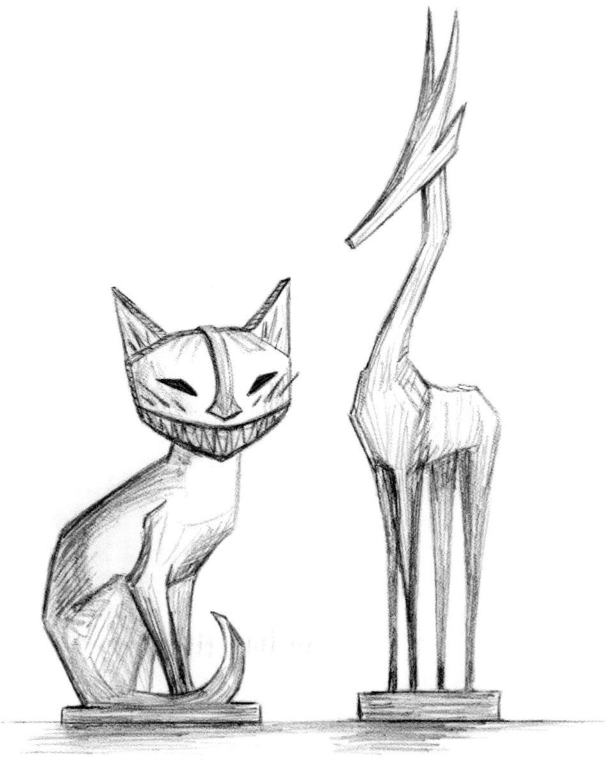

ACKNOWLEDGMENTS

I've been working on this book since 2012. But I would've given up a long time ago if I was doing it alone. There are so many amazing people and dear friends in my life who made it possible:

To my agent, Regina Brooks, thank you for all your hard work, especially for spending hours on the phone answering every newbie question I had. You are the best agent I could have hoped for, and I'm honored to be a part of the Serendipity Literary Agency family.

My deepest thanks to everyone at Scholastic—to David Levithan and Olivia Valcarce for connecting with my vision from the start. To my editor, Lisa Sandell, for your kindness, patience, and encouragement. To creative director Elizabeth Parisi and designer Omou Barry, thank you for turning my words and pictures into such a beautiful book. And thanks to the rest of the Scholastic team, especially the sensitivity reader, copy editors, and marketing and publicity teams.

While the fantasy world in this book is inspired by the kingdoms of West Africa of the tenth through sixteenth centuries, it is not meant to be an accurate representation of any specific group in the past or present. I am indebted to the work of Robin Walker, Zeinab Badawi, Cheikh Anta Diop, Michael A. Gomez, Isaac Samuel, and many others for their expertise in West African history. I owe deep gratitude to the West African storytellers who have created and retold so many wonderful stories full of wit, ingenuity, memorable characters, and sharp observations of life that

remain relatable even today. The firsthand accounts of fourteenth-century explorer Ibn Battūta were also invaluable, as were the works of ʻAbd al-ʻAzīz al-Bakrī and ʻAbd al-Rahmān al-Saʼdī. Lastly, a huge thank-you to Dr. Ysamur Flores-Peña's African Art History class, for opening my eyes to the histories that I had never been taught in school before.

To each of my patrons, and especially Mathew Barnes, Traci Briery, John Carney, Anastasia Dodd, Aaron Flake, Ashley Huntley, Jesse Kersey, Dustin Luce, Charissa McClain, Sarah Richey, Jada Rowland, David Sullivan, and Aubrey Sweeney. Your generous support made this book possible and made me feel less alone, in what is usually a lonely creative process.

To every single person who stopped by my table at WonderCon, Long Beach Comic Con, Emerald City Comic Con, Denver Pop Culture Con, DesignerCon, and Gen Con, or who followed my work on this project

through social media over the years. Your enthusiasm for my art kept me going every time I doubted myself. To Asma Kamara—even though I ended up going in a different direction with Afia, I will always be grateful to you for being the original muse when she was still called Alice.

To my dear friends and cohosts on the *Painted in Color* podcast, Lauren Brown and Eric Wilkerson—I am a better person for knowing both of you; thank you for all your help and support on this book. To the rest of my friends, beta readers, mentors, and fellow artists—Shreya Shetty, Tom Bagshaw, Jana Schirmer, Linda Abramson, Shof Coker, Iain McCaig, Armand Baltazar, Greg Manchess, Irene Gallo, Mark Burstein, David F. Walker, Katherine Lo, Marshall Vandruff,

and everyone else who so generously gave their time to help me. Whether you read my draft once or a million times, cheered me on, patiently did paint-overs for me, or were brutally honest about what worked and what didn't, I am indebted to each and every one of you.

To my partner, Doug—I couldn't have done this without you. Your love and support is everything to me. To Angela DiTerlizzi and Tony DiTerlizzi—I can't thank you enough for your enthusiasm from the start, and for your wisdom and generosity along the way. Thank you to Ellen Goldsmith-Vein and the Gotham Group team for all your hard work and patience.

A mamá y papá—gracias por todo lo que han labu-rado y sacrificado para llegar a este país, donde logramos vivir nuestros sueños. A toda mi hermosa familia en

Argentina, España, e Italia—los quiero mucho a todos.

To my twin sister, Barbra, my first and dearest friend. Writing about these three sets of siblings helped me understand you better, and I hope reading about them helped you to understand me a little better too. If there were ever any doubt of how much I love you, I hope this story makes it clear.

And to you, dear reader. I wrote about fear and curiosity because it's something that I still grapple with in my life and my art. Making this book has taught me, more than any other piece of art that I've created, that growth lies on the other side of fear. And that curiosity, at least for me, is synonymous with life. I hope this story resonates with you, and perhaps helps you to reconnect with the people you love and the things you may have lost along the way.

SKETCHBOOK

PROCESS ART FROM 2012–2024

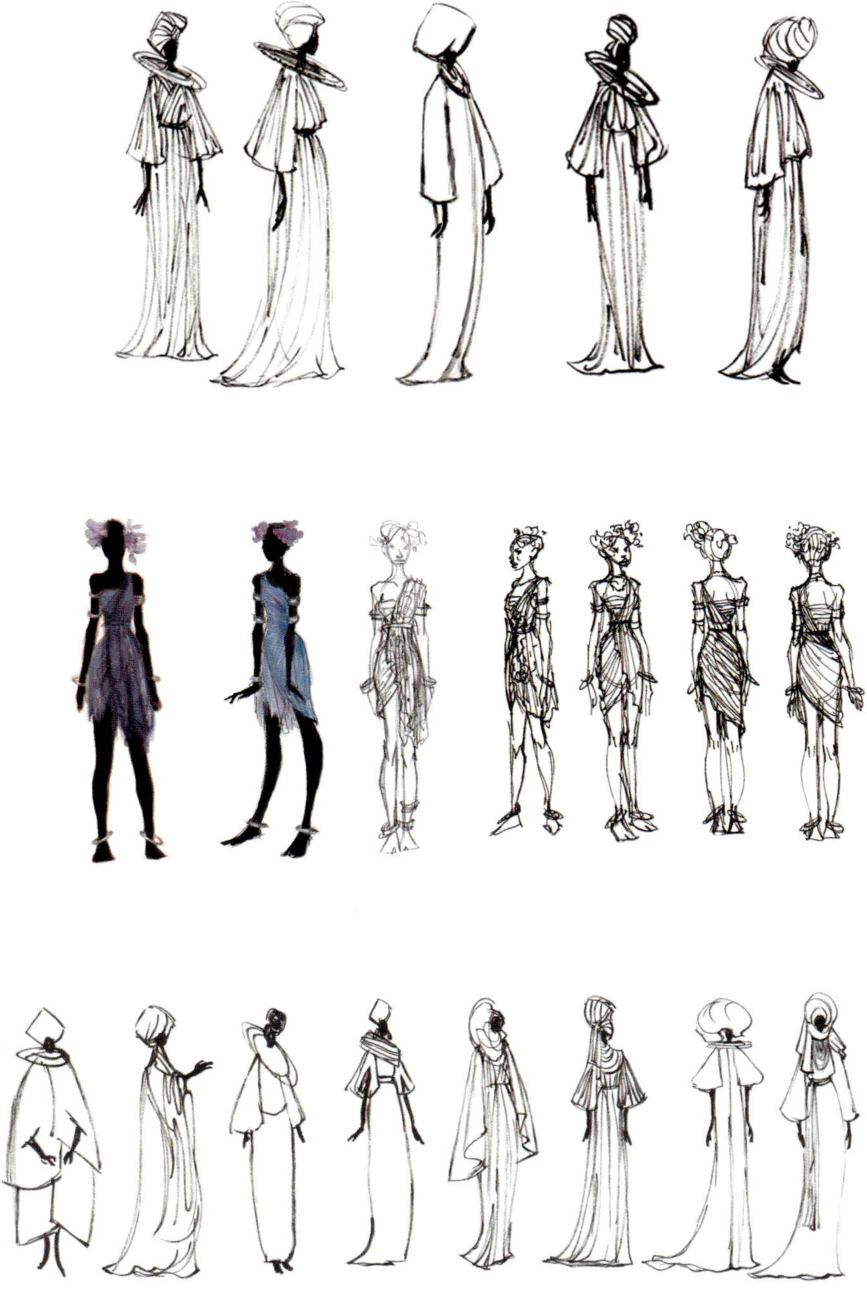

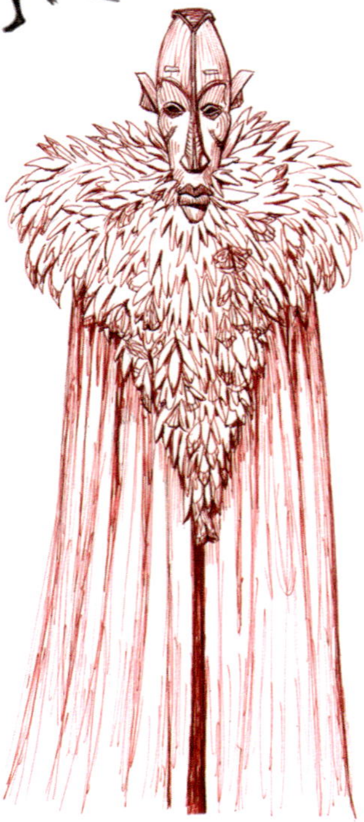

ABOUT THE AUTHOR

Mia Araujo is an Argentine American artist and author, born and raised in Los Angeles. She paints traditionally and creates escapist fantasy stories about the magical connection between humans and nature.

In 2007, she graduated as valedictorian from Otis College of Art and Design, with a BFA in illustration and a minor in creative writing. She has shown her work in prominent galleries in the US and around the world, and has illustrated for Penguin Random House, Wizards of the Coast, HBO, and *The Washington Post*.

She also cohosts *Painted in Color*, a BIPOC art podcast.

When she is not painting or writing, Mia enjoys watching fútbol and filling every sketchbook she can find. Her debut illustrated novel, *Afia in the Land of Wonders*, is a blend of her passions for visual storytelling and prose, a project that she has dedicated more than a decade to crafting. Visit her online at art-by-mia.com.